KNIGHTS OF WARSAW

Shalom Morgan,

D.E.

D.E. CUMMINGS

KNIGHTS OF WARSAW

A NOVEL

Tate Publishing & *Enterprises*

This novel is a work of fiction. However, several names, descriptions, entities, and incidents included in the story are based on the lives of real people.

The opinions expressed by the author are not necessarily those of Tate Publishing, LLC.

Published by Tate Publishing & Enterprises, LLC
127 E. Trade Center Terrace | Mustang, Oklahoma 73064 USA
1.888.361.9473 | www.tatepublishing.com

Tate Publishing is committed to excellence in the publishing industry. The company reflects the philosophy established by the founders, based on Psalm 68:11,
"The Lord gave the word and great was the company of those who published it."

Cover design by Lance Waldrop
Interior design by Stefanie Rooney

Published in the United States of America

ISBN: 978-1-61566-472-6
1. Fiction, Historical
2. History, Holocaust
09.11.19

This book is dedicated to my father,

Donald Roy Schustereit (1935–2006),

whose love for history made me a better person.

Acknowledgments

A very special thank you to the gifted members of my writing group, Roy Vann, Robby Castillo, Liz Gill, and Darlene Houseman. I hear each of your voices in my head every time I sit down to write! Roy, yours tells me to dig for unique details. Robby, yours chimes in at the end of a paragraph or scene and reminds me to make smooth transitions. Liz, when I've deleted something for the umpteenth time, yours whispers, "Simplicity can be effective." And Darlene, yours is always asking, "What does it smell like?" or "How would it feel if you touched it?" In a writer's world, hearing voices can be a good thing!

Thank you to Don Teter, a pillar in Baytown's Jewish community. You have been a tremendous source of help and encouragement.

Your voice, Rabbi Segal, is a righteous voice of truth. Thank you for the amazing foreword.

Kudos to all of my sixth-grade students at Cedar Bayou Junior High. Thank you for being my first audience.

Richard, Elsa, Arlene, and Jim: Bless you, friends! You've been loyal advocates.

Every woman needs a sister. I was blessed with one through marriage. Thank you, Susan, for the inspiring e-mails.

And last but not least, thank you to my husband, Keith, and my boys, Ian and Bryon. You had me published long before I dared to dream of it!

Table of Contents

Foreword 11
Risky Business 15
Sanctuary 21
Righteous Anger 30
A Bittersweet Celebration 37
Lighter Hearts and Pockets 46
Finding Hope 54
Court Is in Session 64
Rumors 78
A Midnight Rendezvous 89
The Sweetness of God 97
Anticipation 102
United in Purpose 109
Connections 115
The Path of Defiance 119
Divided Loyalties 122
The Chosen 127

Better than Diamonds 130
Dark Rooms 134
Voices 139
Never Enough 143
A Light on the Other Side of the Dark 148
Gone 153
The Belly of the Wolf 158
The Stalker 160
A Stirring in the Cemetery 165
False Security 170
The Wolves Within 175
Whispers on the Wind 180
As the Spit Flies 185
More Risky Business 187
The Charade 192
Hallowed Moments 197
Secrets 202
Tragedy and Triumph 209
Reflections 211
What's True about this Story? 217
Glossary 223
Bibliography 225

Foreword

If anyone would ask the average American, *What do you think the following people have in common: David Irving, author and self-proclaimed historian; Arthur Butz, professor of electrical engineering at Northwestern University; Mahmoud Ahmadinejad, president of Iran; James Keegstra, Canadian high school teacher; Roeland Raes, vice president of one of Belgium's largest political parties (the Vlaams Belang); Mahmoud Abbas, president of the Palestinian Authority; Mohammed Mahdi Akef, the leader of the Egyptian Muslim Brotherhood; Revilo P. Oliver, retired University of Illinois classics teacher; and Robert Faurisson, the recipient of a PhD in literature from the University of Lyon?* most people would possibly reply, "I haven't the slightest idea," or they might say, "They all seem to be highly educated," or they might reply with a question—"Do they really have anything in common?"

However, the answer to this question would be: Yes, they all have one thing in common—they are Holocaust deniers. They all claim that there *never* was a Nazi systematic mass murder of 6,000,000 Jews in Europe during World War II. At most, they claim it was merely a few hundred thousand Jews who perished during World War II but not 6,000,000, and most of these deniers add that the vast majority of these Jews died because of disease but not at the hands of Hitler and his Nazi hordes.

This propaganda has spread so much over Canada, England, France, Italy, Sweden, and so many other nations, and the U.S. too, that thirteen countries have actually legislated the preaching of Holocaust denial as illegal: Austria, Belgium, Czech Republic, France, Germany, Israel, Lichtenstein, Lithuania, Luxembourg, Poland, Portugal, Romania, and Switzerland. These nations are European nations, most of whom experienced firsthand the extermination of thousands of Jews during World War II. They feel insulted that Holocaust deniers, who are really anti-Semites, should preach falsehoods about a tragedy they saw with their own eyes.

There were 16,000,000 Jews in the world in November 1938 when the Nazis bore down upon the Jews and initiated what has come to be called the Holocaust. The Nazis burned synagogues in Germany, destroyed Jewish stores, arrested Jews, forcibly placed Jews in concentration camps, and also killed Jews—simply because they were Jews. By the time the war was over in Europe in May 1945, 6,000,000 Jews had been slain, slaughtered, butchered, and liquidated. The Nazis did this with efficiency—shooting them, gassing them, cremating them—in ways previously unimaginable.

The number 6,000,000 to most people is simply a number because no names are attached to that number. It is merely a small object consisting of seven integers. However, if one would say to himself, *Let me think of that number as* 6,000,000 *Jews, with one Jew being killed every second of the day,* then that number would take on a realistic value because counting one murdered Jew a second, it would take 69 days, 10 hours, 40 minutes, and 1 second to count all the Jews who were viciously and intentionally eliminated by the Nazis during World War II.

In fact, in December 1991, the governing council of the American Historical Association, the nation's largest and oldest professional organization for historians, unanimously approved a statement condemning the Holocaust denial movement by stating, "*No* [my emphasis] serious historian questions that the Holocaust took place."

Later, in 1994, The American Historical Association reaffirmed its position in a press release that said, "The association will not provide a forum for views that are, at best, a form of academic fraud."

D.E. Cummings, in her book, *Knights of Warsaw,* has attempted to take one true incident of the Holocaust and develop a historical novel. She admits that she has embellished the story, adding fiction to reality, but the basic premise of the Holocaust remains.

Ms. Cummings does not hide the brutality of the Nazis. On the contrary, she exposes it. There were 9,000,000 Jews in Europe when Hitler came to power. Hitler and his hordes and followers eliminated two-thirds of them, 6,000,000. And if the Allies had not beaten him in 1945, he would have achieved his goal of terminating the lives of the other one-third too.

Cummings has written an important book about Nazi cruelty, Jewish suffering, the desire to live on, the pride of standing up to Nazi savagery, the unbelievable brutality of an entire nation and its cohorts and associates, and the determination of a group of poorly armed, poorly nourished, constantly hounded Jews in the ghetto to proclaim, *Yes, we know we are going to be killed, but we will die fighting with our bare fists, if that is necessary.*

Cummings's book is a thumbing of her nose to all the anti-Semitic Holocaust deniers, who are even today attempting to kill the Jews of the Holocaust a second time and whitewash the foul and obscene, impure and filthy reputation of Adolf Hitler (may his memory be erased).

Rabbi Jack Segal
Rabbi Emeritus, Beth Yeshurun Congregation
Houston, Texas

Risky Business

Over the wall, through holes,
And past the guard,
Through the wires, ruins, and fences,
Plucky, hungry, and determined,
I sneak through, dart like a cat.

A small, shadowy figure wriggled through a hole under the massive brick wall. She emerged on the free side and was grateful for the evening fog. It would make her task easier; smuggling was a risky business—risky but necessary.

She'd adjusted to the cramped quarters at the orphanage. She'd learned to tolerate the incessant noise. Even the absence of a real toilet was bearable. But living with gnawing hunger was miserable.

Hunger was a relentless predator. It stalked its victims, driving them into a desperate frenzy. Ration coupons bought a daily serving of bread for each registered Jew, but any additional food had to be acquired through extraordinary means. It was this reality that had forced Rachel Kremer to become a smuggler at the early age of thirteen.

The first stop on Rachel's route was the trash bins at the back of the produce mart, four blocks from the ghetto. Here, she sometimes found wilted bits of vegetables or bruised fruit. Such substandard food was deemed unfit to satisfy the dining standards of the German officers and *Schutzstaffel,* or SS, guards in Warsaw.

"Ssssstt," hissed Rachel as she stomped on a bald tail. The hungry rodent scurried off to a nearby hole and waited. Rachel dug through the bins, feeling for edible treasures. She thanked the stars for their favor and pocketed four small potatoes that had sprouted eyes, a handful of wrinkled carrots, and two shriveled apples.

The sound of a muffled sneeze jolted her finely tuned instincts, and in one deft movement, Rachel was out of sight. Melting into her surroundings had become as instinctual as breathing.

A grimy, barefoot boy stepped through the curtain of fog. He pilfered through the bins with a quiet urgency, unaware of the wary eyes that watched him. He emerged empty-handed while tears, tainted with hopelessness, coursed their way down his hollow cheeks. Rachel closed her eyes until the familiar twinge of sympathy faded. Visions of the emaciated faces of her fifty-seven siblings overruled any empathy she felt for a stranger—even a Jewish stranger. The boy trudged on.

Rachel's next stop was the neighborhood Catholic church. *I wonder what Sister Agnes has left for me tonight.* The church's groundskeeper had been a regular customer at her parents' small nursery. She kept the flower beds and small garden in beautiful condition. Planting, weeding, fertilizing, and pruning were a means of cultivating the soul for the devoted nun. In the midst of the gloomy, war-torn landscape, the vibrant colors of the plants and flowers nurtured the wounded spirits of passersby.

When Jewish businesses had been confiscated by the Nazis, Sister Agnes came to Rachel's house to buy seeds and supplies. And then the noose around the Jewish neck had tightened. Homes were seized, shops were closed, lives were destroyed, and Warsaw's four hundred thousand Jews were herded into a three-and-a-half-square-mile area surrounded by a ten-foot brick wall.

Sister Agnes had cried the last time she visited the Kremer family. Mingled with her tears of sadness and compassion were the words of a solemn promise. She vowed that Rachel and her family would not be forgotten.

"I will do everything within my power to help you, just as the Lord God provided nourishing manna for Moses and his people while they journeyed through the desert."

And she was true to her word. Every Friday, Rachel found a package of food carefully wrapped and hidden in the compost pile that served as fertilizer for the church garden.

Fond memories of Passover celebrations surfaced as Rachel dug through the musty mixture: Grandpa David hiding the *afikomen* for the youngest family member to find, a triumphant five-year-old Rachel holding the wrapped matzo, crumbs raining down on her head, and a picture of Shimmer, the butterfly created with a set of paints, her prize for finding the bundle of unleavened bread.

How can butterflies and Hitlers exist in the same world? Confusion overwhelmed her thoughts and brought tears to her coffee-brown eyes. *Maybe Sister Agnes knows.* Rachel swept the question into a remote corner of her mind and continued digging.

The familiar feeling of burlap lifted her somber mood. *Sister Agnes calls this an offering. Thank you, God, for nuns and their offerings.* Rachel pulled out the manna bag and was leveling out the compost when the distant bark of a dog alarmed her. She dropped to her knees and draped the roomy gray coat over her head and body. Her heart pounded against her chest bones while she crouched, her forehead flush with the cold ground. *Darkness, my loyal friend, keep me safe,* she prayed. She waited several minutes before daring to move.

The barking subsided, but her quaking did not. She glanced in every direction as she hid the bag, then slipped out of the churchyard. The night was still young, and normally she would have continued to forage, but the blanket of fog was beginning to lift, and in Rachel's experience, barking dogs were never benign. They were always connected to a pair of black boots, a rifle, and a helmet.

"Back to the ghetto," she whispered to the darkness.

The September moon, free from the oppressive fog, illuminated the filthy wall like a spotlight on a stage—one more enemy for Rachel to elude. But unlike the Germans, the silver light of the moon had no evil intentions. She hid behind a small hill of dusty rubble and considered her options.

Both watchtowers positioned next to the thick iron gates were occupied—two SS guards in each. Jewish policemen were stationed inside the ghetto at strategic points. The stings from the clubs of both were equally painful, but somehow the pain from the clubs of her own people seemed to last longer. Rachel was in no hurry to make her move. Eavesdropping on the talkative guards was often profitable, and tonight was no exception.

"This ale is especially good," said the younger SS soldier in the tower nearest Rachel, "but I dare not drink another drop! I must remain beyond reproach if I am to be promoted. Vigilance and loyalty at all times."

"Yes, my boy, you are right on all points," the squatty elder one agreed. "I think we will serve it at the wedding. Only the finest for my daughter and son-in-law-to-be." The gruff, familiar voice of the elder made Rachel seethe. "Frankenstein" was a powerful SS leader, known for his occasional "strolls" through the ghetto. The ruthless, bloodthirsty fiend brandished his revolver and shot anyone at an open window. To the devil's delight, he murdered babies in their strollers too. Such brutality often made Rachel feel that the God of the Jews had forsaken her and her people.

"It's been more than a week since I've taken a nice, long walk," he declared. "I think the exercise and the target practice will do me some good!" The two Germans continued to amuse one another with bigoted comments about the *Jewish filth* they were required to herd.

The blistering hate in their words scalded Rachel's spirit. But they didn't paralyze her. And they didn't cloud her judgment. They were both preoccupied with their idle conversation, and that would work in her favor. She mumbled a quick prayer—"Thank you, God of the Jews, for German ale"—and made her decision.

She inched her way along the cold ground toward the manhole cover. *Through the sewers once again,* she thought. But this time, she was returning with more than just her small treasure of food. Rachel was armed with a warning.

Sanctuary

"And King Matt generously rewarded his knights for protecting their kingdom," concluded the beloved storyteller. "It's time for bed, my precious gems."

"Doctor Papa, why aren't there any brave knights to protect the Jews?" asked five-year-old Jakob.

Janusz Korczak, doctor and educator, scooped the fragile boy up into his arms and gazed into his hungry eyes. "Suffering gives birth to courage, Jakob. Knights will rise up and fight for Jewish honor, and like the swatted fly, the Germans will be stunned! Isn't that true, Rachel?"

"Absolutely! Doctor Papa is right, Jakob," agreed Rachel. She realized that her guardian, though weary and overworked, had noticed her absence. Her stealth served her well on the streets, but inside the orphanage, little escaped the doctor's keen eye.

Rachel watched the gentle man carry Jakob into the nearest sleeping room, lay him on the dingy mattress, and cover him with a thin sheet.

"Now sleep, my boy, and dream of those brave knights. Your dreams will give them strength."

Jakob snuggled up as close as he could to the four other children on the mattress while the doctor struggled to stand. Months of parceling out more than half of his food rations were taking their toll on the man. Rachel grabbed the doctor's walking stick and dashed to his side. They made their way, arm in arm, back into the gathering room and sat at the table together.

"So, my daring little knight, where have you been? It's twenty minutes past curfew. You know it's not safe to be in the ghetto streets after sundown," admonished Korczak.

Rachel thought before answering. She always figured out a way to avoid telling the doctor a blatant lie. "I visited the broken streetcar again to recite the Kaddish. I dreamed about Father's death again last night. The prayer helps to ease the pain."

It was true. She had visited the streetcar to recite the Kaddish. But sneaking out of the ghetto afterward was not part of her answer. A lie of omission seemed like such a minor offense, given the circumstances. And the look on Stefania Wilczynska's face each time she discovered the surplus food made it worthwhile.

"Dr. K., I overheard two guards talking when I was out. Frankenstein will be walking through the ghetto tomorrow, so we must stay inside and keep everyone away from the windows."

"Have you sounded the alarm, child?"

"Yes, sir. I've spread the word."

"The children will be restless, so we will have to fill the day with stories of King Matt and indoor games."

"The little ones will love it, Dr. K., and maybe it will make Sarah feel better. Listen ... She's crying again tonight. She misses that silkie."

"We have turned this place upside down looking for that thing. It's just not here. Stefa tried to replace it with one of her own silk garments, but she refused it." Korczak shook his head in frustration.

"You know, Dr. K., there's one place we haven't looked. I'll go and check for it while you try to comfort her."

Rachel tiptoed through the largest sleeping room and disappeared into the downstairs broom closet that served as one of the restrooms. The dilapidated building, now home to Rachel and fifty-seven other orphans, had one bathroom downstairs and one upstairs. The area's plumbing had failed a few weeks after Warsaw's Jews were forced into the ghetto. Stefania's solution to the problem was primitive but workable. Two sizable aluminum pails were placed in the broom closets to collect the waste. Emptying the contents in a designated pit was a daily chore for the older orphans. Rachel and seventeen others took the unpleasant task in turn. When Rachel made the trek to the pit, she imagined Hitler buried in the monstrous pile of sewage. Then, slinging sludge became a satisfying job.

A rug was attached to a door underneath the pail that led to an underground bunker. The Germans had allowed the building of such rooms so the Jews could hide from Allied bombing. This protection was a ruse designed by the enemy to confuse their prey. The confusion made the torment all the more glorious. But the Germans never figured the ingenuity of the oppressed into their wicked plans. Over time, the bunkers would evolve into a vital network for Jewish defense.

Korczak and Stefania had developed what the youngest orphans thought was a fire drill. Their faithful guardians believed in preserving innocence as long as possible. Stefania had meticulously planned every detail of the drill, and thus far, fortune and the stench that came from the broom closet had kept them safely hidden during many raids.

Rachel pushed the waste container aside and flipped the end of the rug over. She opened the trap door and climbed down the ladder into the dark, dank room. Her right foot slid on something slick, and she fell to her knees. She smiled at her luck when she felt the culprit. It was the silky slip, little Sarah's only keepsake from her dead mother. It had been dropped and left behind during the previous drill. Rachel stuffed the treasure into her coat pocket and climbed out of the bunker. She emerged from the closet and quietly made her way to Sarah's mattress. She knelt down, removed the tiny girl's thumb from her mouth, and gently placed the silken bundle in the crook of her arm.

"You are a gem, Rachel," whispered Korczak. "Now we can all get some sleep."

"I'll sit with her for a few more minutes. You go on to bed," urged Rachel. She waited until she was sure he was in bed then headed for the kitchen to unload her goods.

Sister Agnes's offering for the week was a chunk of Swiss cheese. It was a beautiful, mouthwatering sight. Rachel couldn't remember the last time she had eaten cheese, and she was tempted to cut a thick slice for herself.

"No," she decided. "This is also my offering. I won't cut it." She rewrapped the cheese and stuffed all of her findings in the cupboard.

Being a smuggler has created a bizarre mixture of feelings, she thought. *I'm afraid, ashamed, and proud all at the same time.*

Rachel left the kitchen and put her overcoat back in the broom closet. She was tired from the evening venture and from heavy thoughts. Instead of going to her bed upstairs, the weary smuggler made her way back to Sarah. She crawled onto the mattress, snuggled up to her contented friend, and watched as Sarah rubbed the silkie between her thumb and index finger.

Little victories really do make a difference. The thought calmed the relentless growl of her stomach, and she fell into a satisfying sleep.

"Sister, sister, get up," coaxed Sarah. "Stefania says we're having bread soaked in milk for breakfast."

Rachel opened her sleepy eyes and couldn't help but smile at the sight before her. Sarah sat astride her stomach with her hands resting on her hips.

"See my silkie? One of King Matt's knights found it and brought it to me while I was sleeping."

She unfurled the keepsake and dangled it in Rachel's face. Rachel pretended to go back to sleep and then popped up suddenly, bucking the wee rider onto the mattress. Sarah squealed with delight. Laughter, the only medicine in the ghetto, bubbled from the excited child, and Rachel tickled her to prolong the sweet sound.

Rachel helped Stefa serve breakfast in the gathering room. Meals were taken in shifts from youngest to oldest, with Rachel's group eating last. "Milk? How did we get so lucky?"

"Twenty-six cows were smuggled into the ghetto four nights ago. Two guards were paid to look the other way. There is now a pipe system that carries fresh milk to concealed vats. I can get three gallons every Sabbath morning. A little more insurance against death's angel, the *malekhamoves,*" explained Stefania.

The pleasant sound of smacking coming from the flock of three-year-olds was a hopeful melody. Each group of hungry children savored the soggy treat and washed it down with sips of water from their canteens.

Stefania's milky breakfast worked up a merry magic, and after Sabbath prayers, the recreation began. The eight- and nine-year-old boys took turns playing the part of King Matt, and the girls of the same group played the part of Klu Klu, a tomboy princess. In Korczak's story, the two meet when King Matt explores her primitive island.

Rachel joined Sarah at the puppet theater and watched as Jakob played the part of a valiant knight. "We come for you, Hitler! We will swat you like a fly!"

"Who is Hitler, sister?" asked Sarah.

"He is a monstrous man," answered Rachel, "so

full of hate and deceit that there is no room in his heart for love."

"Then I feel sorry for him. I think everyone should know how to love," decided Sarah.

"Yes, they should!" said Rachel, unable to argue with the child's poignant words.

A teacher worked with a group of young girls, teaching them to make dolls from paper. Avram, Joshua, and a few of the other fourteen- and fifteen-year-old boys were using scrap wood to make a pair of doll cradles. Korczak was surrounded by girls and boys of various ages. They were writing a poem for Rosh Hashanah, the Jewish New Year.

The collective noises coming from the assembly hall muffled the sporadic gunfire that reverberated in the streets. They muffled the screams. And they muffled the mournful recitations of the Kaddish, the prayer for the dead.

Korczak, Avram, and Rubin took the younger children upstairs later that afternoon while Rachel and Hannah helped prepare the evening meal.

"Girls, do either of you know how these extra vegetables and cheese found their way into our cupboard?" asked Stefa. Fortunately, she was too busy gathering things to look at the girls when she asked the question. That made lying easier.

"One of the doctor's former students brought them here today," said Rachel. "He seems to have so many connections inside and outside the ghetto."

"Dr. K. is an influential man, ladies. His goodness has made him a very popular person. He is esteemed by the wealthy and the poor. We could not survive without those connections. Would you chop the vegetables, Rachel? And Hannah, would you cut that gorgeous hunk of cheese into sixty-two pieces?"

Yes, the cheese is a wonderful offering. But I'm not sure Sister Agnes would appreciate me lying about where it came from. Rachel shook off the wave of guilt and attacked the carrots first. Then she cut the eyes from the dozen or so shriveled potatoes but left the skin on.

"Skinning a potato is sinful. Children need every vitamin hidden in those skins." Rachel whispered her mother's words while she worked. The memory brought tears to her eyes. She forced them back and grabbed the withered green beans. They were too soft to snap, so she cut them into segments and added them to the pot. Then Hannah came over and dropped something from her hand into the mixture.

"Salt. It was one of the last things I grabbed as I left our apartment to come here. I've been saving it for a special occasion," said Hannah.

"What a nice surprise! Did you grab a hunk of beef too?" joked Rachel.

When the dinner crew finished their tasks, Dr. Korczak blessed the feast and showered words of praise on them. "The meal we eat tonight is made from the fruits of this group's labor. Let us be thankful."

Each shift of hungry children enjoyed a small serving of savory soup, a slice of warm bread, cheese, and an apple wedge. The older orphans were the last to eat. They took small bites, thoroughly enjoying the food and the camaraderie they shared.

"So tell me. Did Stefa wonder where the extra food came from?" asked Avram, a knowing grin on his face.

"Yes, you know she did. And I was the one who had to dream up an answer. I told her that one of Dr. K's former students brought it to us. Tell me, Avram, how is it that you always manage to escape Stefa's questioning?" volleyed Rachel.

"It is my incredible talent for being slippery," he boasted. "Shall I give you lessons, my dear Rachel?"

Grabbing his ear, Rachel teased, "Try and slip away now, you scoundrel!"

Avram yelped like an injured dog, and the oldest orphans laughed until their sides ached.

Rachel reflected on the day as she lay on her mattress that night. She was thankful that the *malekhamoves* had passed over their door, sparing the innocent lives within. The orphanage had thus far been a haven, a sanctuary that sheltered Rachel and the others from much of the brutality and chaos that the German devils unleashed. Twenty-eight Jews, seven of them infants, were murdered that day as Frankenstein strolled through the ghetto. Rachel knew firsthand that such terror inevitably brought desperate, grieving children to the doorstep of the orphanage; she had arrived four months earlier under the same circumstances.

Righteous Anger

A pitiful whimper stirred Rachel from a deep sleep. She sat up, yawned, and started to stand when she realized that the soft cry was coming from a strange girl on the mattress nearest hers. The slender, dark-haired figure shifted restlessly, captive to whatever nightmarish scene played out in her troubled mind. *I wonder what haunts her.* Rachel reached out to calm the girl but decided against it. There was a hint of raw pain in the girl's cry that was uncomfortably familiar.

Rachel lay on her side, her back to the stranger. She covered her ears with her hands and tried desperately to evade the clutches of sleep. But sleep returned, along with her own haunting nightmare.

That Tuesday had been long but productive. Rachel headed home with three small potatoes hidden in her pockets. She pulled the scarf from her head before entering the stairwell of her apartment building and used it to cover her mouth and nose. The corners of the landings had become collection spots for human waste after the building's plumbing failed. The wretched odor usually made her heave but not today. With potatoes in her pockets, it was hardly noticeable. She dashed up the steps and exited the stairwell, eager to present the brown jewels to her waiting mother.

Three eighteen was the last apartment on the left and the last one available when she and her parents had moved into the ghetto five months earlier. They were lucky; some of her friends and their families were living in public buildings. Some were living on the streets.

Rachel was envisioning the steamed potatoes they would have when she heard a dreadful cry. *That sounds like it's coming from our apartment.* She burst through the door and stopped dead in her tracks. Her wild-eyed, frantic father sat in the middle of the living room floor, cradling the limp body of her mother and shouting at the ceiling. "Bring her back! You cannot have her!"

Rachel cast aside the heavy coat and dropped to her knees. "Father, did Mama pass out? Should I get—"

She choked on the words when she noticed the loosened noose around her mother's neck. She stared with eyes that didn't want to see.

The realization of what happened crept into her consciousness like imposing fog. A stream of tears made its way down her dirt-streaked face as she picked up the note.

Please forgive me for leaving you. Ruth was taken to the quarantine building with symptoms of typhus this morning. She and I have worked together at the mill for several weeks now, so it would have only been a matter of time before I came down with it. Then you. I cannot let that happen. Take care of one another and know that my love for you will never die. Rebekah.

Rachel folded the note and was about to offer it to her father when he jumped up and bolted from the apartment. She ran after him but stumbled and fell in the doorway. She turned around, crawled back, and rested her head on her mother's chest. She cried because it would never again rise and fall with the breath of life. She cried because a daughter needed her mother to lead her through certain rites of passage. And she cried because the rest of the world was silent.

A rustling sound startled her. "Father?" Rachel lifted her head and looked around. The door was still open, and a ghostly draft drifted into the room. She reached to close it and noticed her mother's lacy shawl hanging next to the door's frame. Traces of her mother's sweet perfume lingered in the delicate cloth. She held it to her face and breathed in the memory. Then she gently lifted her mother's torso, removed the noose from her bruised neck, and draped the shawl around her head.

"I'll leave the potatoes by the stove and go find Father. It's been a week since we last had a potato."

Rachel's mind was numb. She left the building and made her way up the sad street. The sun was setting, leaving the ghetto shrouded in a dingy dusk.

She was passing a strip of looted shops splattered with swastikas when she heard his voice.

Oliver Kremer stood on top of a broken streetcar and shouted to an attentive crowd. "They starve us! They humiliate us! They rob us of our honor! Find the anger—the righteous anger that simmers below your fear," he implored, "and harness it. Together we can—"

A shot sounded. The passionate voice died abruptly and was replaced by a sinister laugh. Terrified screams rang out. People scattered frantically in every direction. Four more bullets exploded from Frankenstein's gun, each hitting its mark. Rachel dove behind a garbage can. Fear sucked the breath from her lungs and drained the color from her face.

When he passed, she made her move. She scaled the back of the broken streetcar and found her father lying on his back, legs and arms quivering with shock. She lifted his head, positioned it in her lap, and cried, "Father! Father! You can't leave! Mother is waiting for both of us. She has the potatoes ready by now."

Blood streamed from the fatal chest wound. Rachel tore the scarf from her neck and used it to stem the flow. His eyelids fluttered. He tried to utter the words, "Shalom, precious daughter," but the blood that gurgled in his throat drowned the loving farewell.

Spasms of grief shook her body. She sobbed. She wailed. And she hurled curses into the darkness. It was a dangerous thing, her ranting. An invitation for her own death. But the catharsis purged her mind and made room for a healing thought. *Part of you will always be with me.* She placed both of her hands on the sides of his face and began the mourner's prayer. The words of the Kaddish floated on the wind, and heaven cried.

"Magnified and sanctified be the glory of God." Tears for Rebekah Kremer. "In the world created according to his will." Tears for Oliver Kremer. "May his sovereignty soon be acknowledged." Tears for Rachel Kremer, now alone in her hostile world. "During our lives and the life of all Israel." And tears for all Jews suffering under Hitler's oppressive regime. "Let us say: Amen."

Rachel struggled to get her father onto the ground where the undertaker's assistants would find him. She sat by his body and repeated the prayer until sleep swept her away.

It was midnight when a young Jewish policeman on graveyard duty wandered upon a strange sight—a living, breathing child was slumbering in the crook of a dead man's stiffening arm. The officer gasped. The sleeping girl, though taller, looked just like his younger sister.

He stooped and shook her awake. "You must go home. It's not safe out here."

Her anger boiled. "You! You're a traitor. What do you—"

"Shhhh! Do you want to get us both killed?" He glanced about anxiously and then looked at Rachel.

Rachel looked away. *Why did he have to wake me? I would have gladly slept until death arrived.* She turned and glared at him. "I no longer have a home. Both of my parents … " Reality swelled in her throat. "But what do you care? You have no soul. The Germans have bought it!"

The words were like bullets, ripping into his conscience. "Look, I know someone who will shelter you. Children call him the angel of the ghetto."

"The only angel I've seen is the *malekhamoves,*" she said bitterly. "He is everywhere. He has taken my father and my mother, and now he hunts me."

"The man who can help you is a doctor. He could dress that cut on your arm." He held out his hand and waited.

Rachel looked at the wound. A trail of fresh blood trickled down her arm and into her left palm. "I never felt it."

"Will you let me look at it? Before the ghetto, I had started my medical studies."

She whispered a promise in the lifeless man's ear and then took the outstretched hand. "My mother can take potatoes and turn them into the most incredible dishes. You'll have to come to dinner sometime."

"Don't leave me, Father!" The newcomer's cry woke Rachel once again.

She listened with ears that didn't want to hear.

She had no comfort to offer the girl, so she tiptoed across the room and woke Hannah. "The new girl . . . She's crying out. Please come help me. You're so much better with kids our age."

Hannah knelt by the mattress and caressed the stranger's cheek. "Shh, shh, shh, it's okay, now. You are safe. You're with friends."

Rachel sat on her mattress and watched while Hannah tried to wake the restless girl. The scene reminded Rachel of a game of tug of war, with Hannah tugging in one direction and the nightmare pulling from the other. Hannah's compassion prevailed, and the nightmare faded. Within minutes, the girl was coherent, and the three of them were talking.

"Father shielded the baby. And Frankenstein still killed both of them! Bravery serves no purpose in this forsaken ghetto," Elizabeth said, her voice saturated with disgust.

Rachel responded to Elizabeth's lament with an unexpected certainty that surprised all of them. "Acts of courage, like your father's, will someday ignite a righteous fire that will burn with vengeance. His sacrifice will not be forgotten!"

"I hope you're right," said Elizabeth, "and I hope I live to see it."

A Bittersweet Celebration

Rain darkened the dusty street as Rachel and Elizabeth made their way to the meeting place. The trip was on-the-job training for Elizabeth. She had taken an immediate interest in the art of smuggling, and Rachel had volunteered to train her. The dump was inside the ghetto, so this low-risk venture was ideal for her first experience.

"Dr. Korczak has some compassionate Gentile friends that are part of the Polish Underground. They collect trash two days a week using a rented garbage truck. The risky part of their work involves hiding packages of supplies in the piles of trash," explained Rachel.

"What kinds of things do they bring?" asked Elizabeth.

"Letters and food mostly. But Dr. Korczak said that there would be something special in today's delivery. I can't wait to find out what it is."

Elizabeth's eyes widened with intrigue. "How do you keep from getting caught?"

"Certain guards can be bribed if the price is right."

Rachel turned a corner, and her apprentice followed. "Money can be more persuasive than Hitler."

Rachel spotted a man sitting on the sidewalk, his back against the wall of a looted store. His head was tilted slightly upward, and his eyes were wide open. His gaze was fixed and unnatural; any sights his eyes beheld were not of the living world. Rachel hurried to his side. She closed his eyes, began reciting the Kaddish, then proceeded to strip the man of his belongings. Elizabeth stood watching, her mouth agape.

"This coat is thin," noted Rachel, "but it will fit Avram. Last year's coat won't cover his growing arms."

"What on earth are you doing?" asked Elizabeth, looking from side to side to see if anyone was near.

"He no longer needs these things." Rachel checked the pockets. "They can be used by others. It is what he would want."

"How do you know that?"

"Think about it, Elizabeth. It's what you would want. It's what I would want. It's a matter of survival. Inside these walls, feeling sorry for others can get you killed. You must learn to make each choice with that in mind. Now come and help me, please."

"I suppose you're right," conceded Elizabeth. She walked over to the corpse and knelt by Rachel.

"Put on this coat. We can divide the other things between us and carry them in our sacks." Rachel stuffed a pair of mismatched shoes in her bag. "And remember what I said about the snatchers."

"They work quickly and quietly."

Before leaving, Rachel knelt at the man's side once again and repented, "Forgive me, sir, for any harm I've caused you, and may your name be sealed in the Book of Life." Elizabeth whispered the same words.

The Jewish New Year, followed by the ten days of repentance, had not begun, so the request and blessing offered by both girls was premature. But the two children had already learned what many of the adults had not; in the ghetto, rules and customs had to be bent and broken in order to survive.

The grimy dump had once been a city park. Mountains of trash replaced the swings and merry-go-round. Gone was the sweet smell of cotton candy, carried away by the winds of war. A simmering stench had settled in its place. Scurrying rodents raced about in place of frolicking children, and layer upon layer of gloom and despair smothered the cheer that once energized the area.

The guard stationed near the dump was paid to ignore any Jewish children gathering items from the trash piles. His sick daughter and mounting medical bills ensured the ongoing success of this particular smuggling operation.

After a few quick instructions, Rachel and Elizabeth scavenged through the rubbish, potato sacks in hand. The two garbage men were busy loading trash that had been pilfered through numerous times. The devoted members of the underground had also done some unloading; hidden in the various piles were packages marked with a *K*.

In the light of the waning moon, the two girls found eight of these securely wrapped parcels. Elizabeth felt lucky to find the one marked *special* and *delicate*. She held her breath to keep from squealing with delight. Placing the prize carefully on top of the two others, she secured the sack and rejoined Rachel.

"I found three," Elizabeth whispered. "One was marked with the words *special* and *delicate,* so I put it on top."

"Good. The tall one over there told me what's in it," Rachel said, pointing to one of the garbage men. "I'll fill you in on the way back. It's good to know that we Jews have not been completely forgotten."

"What are the men's names?" asked Elizabeth.

"In these times, names are never exchanged."

"Why not?" Elizabeth glanced at the men as they got into the truck.

"If we were caught tonight, God forbid, no amount of torture would produce names. Sometimes not knowing is best," Rachel said. "Now let's head back. You should stay behind me, though. With these bulging sacks, it's not safe to return the way we came. Cover your mouth and nose with your scarf because we're about to travel through the bowels of the ghetto."

Two rugged orphans quietly set aside the heavy manhole cover and climbed out, smelling like the devil's own cesspool. Darkness—friend and guardian of all smugglers—shielded her young charges as they made their way to the back door of their haven.

"That was really disgusting, Rachel. And look, I've got twice as much filth on me. How do you do it?"

"You'll learn every inch of those sewers in a few months. Then you'll know where to step and where not to step. And unless ordered to, no German soldier will follow you in there," explained Rachel. "Now, let's shed these wading pants and get inside."

"What loyal friends I have!" remarked Korczak as he surveyed the contents of the special package. "Look, here is a *shofar* for the Rosh Hashanah celebration. What a beautiful horn! Our New Year celebration will be very special. And here are candles for Yom Kippur, the day of forgiveness. We will transform this gathering room into a synagogue and secretly observe both holidays. The New Year celebration will provide renewed hope, and the Yom Kippur observance purity of heart and soul. The Germans have robbed us of our possessions. They have closed the synagogues and forbidden us to worship openly. But they cannot steal our faith."

In the brief silence that followed, Korczak traced the intricacies of the horn with his finger. Then a spark of defiance danced in the aging man's eyes, and determination strengthened his weary shoulders. "Stefa, can you visit your friend at the mill and ask for extra bread? I will arrange for a cantor to sing for both celebrations. He will be honored. Elizabeth, please inform the Hebrew teacher that we will be celebrating both holidays. Ask her to work on the catalogue of sins listed in the prayer book with all of her classes. I will be inviting a small group of trustworthy people to join us for the services, and I want them to see that my children are well versed in Jewish tradition."

The smuggling business was slow the week before Rosh Hashanah, and without the contribution from Korczak's friends in the Polish Underground, there would not have been any apples for the New Year celebration. Rachel was surprised that his friends knew to send apples.

"They're Gentiles, Dr. K. How did they know we needed apples this week?"

"Many Gentiles are aware of our suffering. Some have risked their lives for us. Others have lost their lives when they were caught helping us. My Christian friends, understanding the importance of religious traditions, have obviously done some research. They are aware of our upcoming holidays and how we observe them. Always remember, Rachel, that we were all created in God's image. He is with us. Through the garbage men and so many others, he is with us. We must remember this when we feel abandoned."

As he talked of the garbage men, Rachel thought of Sister Agnes. She had never really considered the fact that the woman was risking her life. *Sacrifice.* The word floated into her mind and settled there. *How much will be required before this evil passes? How much will be asked of me?*

The New Year was ushered in with peace and reverence. To begin the service, Korczak welcomed the guests and then turned the service over to the cantor. Rachel listened more intently than ever before—forbidden words invited avid listeners.

> On Rosh Hashanah it is inscribed,
> And on Yom Kippur it is sealed,
> How many shall pass away,
> And how many shall be born,
> Who shall live and who shall die.

Rachel thought about her parents and then about her own fate. *This war, this nightmare, is interfering with everyone's fate. It wasn't Mother or Father's time to die.* She wondered about the realities that could seal her own fate. Starvation. Disease. Execution. *I will not die before my time. I—*

The sleeping bundle in her lap shifted, interrupting her thoughts. Rachel looked down at four-year-old Devorah, the latest newcomer. She had been dangerously weak from hunger and dehydration when she arrived. But after two weeks in Stefa's intensive care, she was strong enough to join the others in her age group.

Devorah whimpered, and Rachel smoothed her hair and rubbed her back. She enjoyed helping Stefa with the little ones. And since their numbers had grown to seventy-eight, Stefa was especially grateful for the extra help.

The shofar was blown, and the rich, mellow

sound evoked gasps of delight from every child. The cantor responded, "Let us cry out to God in our times of need."

Devorah's whimpers turned into a pitiful bawl. *We do cry,* thought Rachel. *God's ears must be full by now!* She hummed and rocked, but the orphaned nestling would not be consoled. Stefa came over, took the child, and excused herself from the rest of the service.

The cantor ended the service with a plea for God's compassion. His voice rang out with zeal.

> O Lord, hear my voice when I call; be gracious, and answer me. *It is you that I seek,* says my heart. It is your presence that I crave, O Lord. Hide not your presence from me; reject not your servant. You are my help; do not desert me. Forsake me not, God of my deliverance. Though my father and mother forsake me, the Lord will gather me in and care for me. Teach me your way, O Lord. Guide me on the right path, to confound those who mock me. Deceivers have risen against me, men who breathe out violence. Abandon me not to the will of my foes. Mine is the faith that I surely will see the Lord's goodness in the land of the living. Hope in the Lord and be strong. Hope in the Lord and take courage.

Courage, thought Rachel. *The things that once required courage seem so simple now. Learning to ride my bike. Reading aloud in front of my classmates for the first time. Reciting the four questions at the Passover meal. These days, courage seems as scarce as food. The Germans have—*

"Rachel, come and see the surprise! We have apples, bread, and honey!" Sarah grabbed one hand, and Devorah grabbed the other. Both of the small hands were already sticky with the golden goodness.

Adults and children alike dipped an apple and bread slice into the honey. This tasty custom was an invocation for a sweet year. As she listened to the traditional farewells between adults—*May God inscribe you and your loved ones for a healthy and happy new year*—Rachel doubted the existence of anything sweet or happy outside the walls of the orphanage.

Lighter Hearts and Pockets

"Between now and Yom Kippur, let us all seek forgiveness from those we have wronged. And may our acts of kindness inspire hope in others." Korczak's words marked the beginning of the ten days of penitence. Pardons were given and received. Blessings engendered blessings. And like golden sunlight that caresses the tender bloom, grace anointed the melancholy spirit.

"Dr. K. said that we each have to look for our own opportunity to bless someone. Are you sure this will count for both of us?" asked Rachel as she and Avram walked past the dump.

"Why wouldn't it?" he replied. "I'm taking her this bunch of rotten planks to use for firewood, and you're giving her a book. Aunt Giena can read the book one evening by the fire. By my count, that's two separate blessings."

"I wish I could have found something besides Charles Dickens's *A Christmas Carol.* It was written for a Christian audience."

"It's a classic, and anybody who appreciates literature will love the story. And when you think about it, it's the perfect Yom Kippur story, even if it was written by a Christian. Scrooge repents. He gets the opportunity to right his wrongs. And that's what Yom Kippur is all about."

"You've convinced me. Now, where did you say Giena—"

"The rich are dissolving! All are equal! In the ghetto, all are equal!" sang a whimsical voice. The slim body belonging to the voice darted in front of Rachel and Avram. He gave them a smug smile and then disappeared as suddenly as he had appeared.

"How odd!" exclaimed Rachel. "Who is he?"

"You've never seen Rubinstein before? He's the mad jester of the ghetto, a self-appointed entertainer. Curious, but bizarre."

"I think that his hunger has gone to his head!"

"Here it is. Aunt Giena's apartment is in this building. You'll need to watch your step as we climb the stairs. People use anything for a toilet these days." Avram opened the door, and the stench assaulted them both; sour body odor, stale urine, and the wretched smell of disease brought tears to their eyes.

Rachel adjusted her scarf so it covered her mouth and nose. "We are fortunate, Avram, to live in such a clean place. I should thank Stefa and Dr. K. for their hard work."

As Avram knocked on the door, Rachel remembered to pull her scarf down. "Yes?" answered a voice, wary and iced with fear.

"It's Avram, Aunt Giena. Avram and a friend. Can we come in?"

A tall woman with drawn features opened the door. She grabbed his hand, pulled him through, and quickly shut the door behind Rachel. "Of course, child. Forgive my hesitation. Our world is full of wolves these days. Samuel, come and see our nephew." The woman turned to Rachel. "And who is this pretty friend of yours?"

Avram put his hand on Rachel's back. "Aunt Giena and Uncle Samuel, meet Rachel—Rachel Kremer."

"You have good taste in friends, my boy," remarked Samuel as he held his hand out for Rachel to shake.

"What brings you to this part of the ghetto?" asked Giena. "It isn't safe to travel these streets. There are guards and snatchers, informants and wolves. Did anyone follow you?"

"We were careful, Aunt Giena." Avram turned and winked at Rachel. "Both of us can be slippery when necessary. We came to make a special delivery." He walked over to the empty fireplace and set the bundle of wood down. "This wood will make a toasty fire. When I was gathering it, I remembered that you love to sit by a fire. We stay warmer in the orphanage than you do in this drafty apartment building."

"What a treat, Avram! How kind of you to think of me. Samuel, can you believe it? Our nephew is a resourceful boy. My sister would be so proud of him. Firewood!" she exclaimed. "We've only had two or three fires this season. Wood is scarce. I will think of you when we use it. Now, come and sit down so we can visit properly."

Rachel sat down on the worn sofa. She looked back at the fireplace while Avram chatted and noticed that the mantel had been torn from the wall. *Another sacrifice,* thought Rachel as she looked at the small bed of cold ashes. She had heard that people who were desperate for warmth were cutting up furniture to burn.

"And when I told Rachel that you loved literature, she insisted on bringing you a book to read while you sit by the fire." Avram nudged her with his elbow.

"Yes, the book." Rachel handed the book to Giena and apologized. "I'm sorry. My mind wandered. Our library at the orphanage is a small one. Most of the books are for the younger children. But Dr. Korczak believes in the classics. I hope you like it."

"You children are exceptional. I wish there was something I could ... Wait, there is. Samuel, go get these children a lemon drop each." The man smiled as he got up. "Samuel managed to sneak out several bags of candy before they plundered the store."

Samuel returned, his face beaming with pride. Rachel and Avram rose to meet him. "My favorite piece of candy. Just the right amount of sweet and sour blended into a perfect teardrop. Enjoy."

"Thank you," said Rachel. "I can't remember the last time I had a piece of candy."

"Well, we need to get home. Stefa will be looking for us. Take care of each other and come to see us when you get the chance. Visitors are always welcome." Avram hugged Giena and exchanged a warm handshake with Samuel.

As soon as Giena let them out and closed the door, she questioned Samuel. "That was Avram, wasn't it? It's been so long since we've seen him. What if . . . ?"

As they made their way home, the late afternoon sun began a slow descent. Golden beams of sunlight colored the drab streets. Avram and Rachel walked at a steady, determined pace. They pretended to be anxious, even though they were comforted by each other's presence. They concealed the delight created by the lemony sensation. The guise was necessary; a calm, happy Jew stood out and became a target. Conversation was minimal, but Rachel couldn't help asking, "Is your aunt okay?"

"You must have heard what she said after she closed the door."

"Yeah, I did."

"My aunt was always the nervous type. Never really able to relax. I noticed that she was restless during the visit, even when we were sitting on the couch. It seems that this war has made her nervous condition worse."

Rachel started to ask if he had noticed the missing mantel but settled on another question instead. "I'm glad we made that delivery. Aren't you?"

On Yom Kippur, the orphanage once again doubled as a synagogue. Supporters of the home came to observe the day of forgiveness. Korczak and the cantor had planned an abbreviated but meaningful service involving many of the children.

After a brief welcome by Korczak, Joshua and Hannah lit the candles to begin the evening service. The cantor sang the opening meditations and then, together with the audience, recited the Kol Nidrei. Rachel always marveled at this particular prayer. It was one that offered a year's worth of forgiveness in advance.

Twenty-two children, including Sarah and Devorah, were involved in the middle portion of the ceremony. They lined up without incident, and then, guided and cued by the Hebrew teacher, each child recited a sin from the lengthy list.

Sarah was the first in line. Her sweet little voice made her seem incapable of committing the sin that had been assigned to her. "We have sinned against you by being heartless." Her words were loud and clear, and when she finished, she took her place at the end of the line.

When the last child had recited the last sin on the list, all of them spoke in unison, "For all these sins, forgiving God, forgive us, pardon us, grant us atonement."

That list covers everything, Rachel thought, *even taking the personal belongings from a dead man.*

When the children sat down, Korczak got up. In

his speech, he tried to reassure the children that they would live to see happier times. He ended with a small part of the twenty-seventh Psalm. "Mine is the faith that I surely will see the Lord's goodness in the land of the living. Hope in the Lord and be strong. Hope in the Lord and take courage."

A well-designed reception followed the service. Korczak had splurged on refreshments for the event. He knew that if his plan worked, it would pay off.

That morning, children had been given paper and pencil and instructed to write about their acts of kindness. Instead of putting their names on the pages, they put their ages. In doing this, they would not be guilty of boasting. The finished reports were turned in to Stefa.

When everyone had received his portion of the refreshments, Korczak asked the guests to return to the gathering room for a special presentation. He stood in front of the audience, leaning heavily on his walking stick. "In these times of uncertainty and despair, we need the sustaining power of hope. Over the past ten days, these children have done their part in meeting that need. Listen as Stefa Wilczynska elaborates."

Stefa rose to the occasion and played her part well. "Says a ten-year-old boy, 'This week I gave my potato pancake to the old man who begs by the streetcar. He is too old to work, so he doesn't get ration coupons.'

"Says a six-year-old girl, 'There is a woman who lives on the sidewalk next to the barber's old shop. She has a new baby who is always cold and hungry. I gave her my blanket, the one with the bunnies on it, to wrap the baby in. I'm not sure why, but she cried when I gave it to her.'

"Says a fifteen-year-old boy, 'My aunt and uncle live in a drafty apartment building. Aunt Giena is always anxious and fearful. But a fire seems to calm her. I remembered this as I was out gathering wood to burn. We are warmer here in the orphanage, so I delivered an armful of wood to her on Tuesday. She was delighted.'"

With a fierce sense of pride, Stefa read seventy-eight accounts of kindness shown. Then she ended with a thoughtful benediction. "Help us, oh Lord, to learn from these children. May their benevolence inspire us to renew our own commitments to those who are less fortunate."

A lengthy round of applause followed her last words. Korczak walked up to Stefa and accompanied her to the door. He stood on one side, and she stood on the other as the guests filed out. Warm farewells were exchanged, and each guest left with a lighter heart. And pocket.

Finding Hope

Rachel slipped into the frigid night, eager for some time alone—eager, but terrified. Smuggling was a dark art; it meant inviting death yet willing survival. She knew that she was courting death every time she ventured out. She'd heard the stories; children caught, tortured, and killed in their desperate quests for food. And some nights, the fear of meeting that same fate kept her inside. Sleep was usually fitful on those nights.

Inevitably, she would travel her route in a dream and get caught every time. Her captor would grab the meager morsels she'd scavenged, throw them to the ground, and urinate on them. Then Rachel would wake up, his demonic laugh still ringing in her ears. Shaken by the nightmare, Rachel would postpone her business ventures for several days. But when hunger turned the usual night whimpers of the little ones into pitiful wailing, she was driven beyond her fear and returned to the dark streets of Warsaw.

A sudden gust of frosty wind blasted Rachel, causing her to gasp. It was October, and winter was descending upon Poland. The brutal season promised misery, especially for the Jews. The first freeze ushered in additional worries for Korczak and his small staff. As a result of their concerns, a new holiday was born: Exchange Day. All of the orphans were instructed to turn in articles of clothing they had outgrown. Classes were cancelled, and an entire day was set aside for measuring, fitting, and swapping clothes. The gathering room looked like a department store, complete with wee ones laughing and diving in and out of the piles. Mixed into each stack of dirty, tattered clothes were a few new pieces, compliments of the Underground. By sunset, each child had been fitted with two sets of clothes, a scarf, cap, and mittens. For the holiday finale, the children lined up from youngest to oldest and paraded through the downstairs area, singing their orphanage anthem:

White and brown and black and yellow,
Mix the colors with one another.
People are still brothers and sisters
Of one father and one mother!

After a second hearty round of the tune, Rachel had ducked into the broom closet, grabbed the shabby overcoat, and left for work.

Becoming one with the darkness, Rachel adjusted the scarf around her neck and headed for the hole under the east ghetto wall. Fate intervened, though, and she never made it. She was passing the barbershop when she heard it: an unmistakable cry, faint but persistent.

I'm going to ignore whatever this is. I'll walk right past it.

Rachel had learned to ignore the desperate cries of people outside of the orphanage, but this cry was different; she was inexplicably drawn to whatever helpless creature was making it.

As she neared the deserted shop, Rachel tripped over the dead woman's legs. Suppressing a scream, she instinctively rolled into a tight ball, covered her head with her hands, held her breath, and waited for the dreaded sound of guard boots slapping the sidewalk.

Thankfully, she heard nothing but the weak cry. She righted herself and inched forward, her thoughts racing. *I know what this is. Why can't I just walk away? I need to work tonight. And there are enough hungry mouths waiting back at home. Why me?*

When Rachel reached the lifeless woman, the crying stopped momentarily. But when her hand met a cold, bare breast, she knew her instincts were right. Trapped in the mother's stiffening arm was a baby. Rachel jerked her hand back, and the motion triggered more crying from the starving infant. She covered her ears with her hands and sat paralyzed by indecision. Finally, it was the memory of her stillborn sibling that moved her to act.

In one fluid move, Rachel lifted the baby and the thin blanket he was wrapped in from his lifeless mother and swaddled him in her overcoat. Then, laying the bundle at her side, she started to remove the woman's clothes when a vision of her own mother's lifeless body crept into her mind. Claiming valuable clothing from a corpse was routine, but this time, she just couldn't. She whispered the Kaddish then picked up the bundle and returned to the orphanage.

“Where did you say you found him?” asked Korczak.

“I found him right next to his mother’s body. They were just outside of the barber’s old shop. You know, the one by the streetcar.”

“This boy is a fighter,” declared Korczak as he examined the newest orphan. “He can’t be more than two months old. It’s nothing short of a miracle that he’s alive. I wonder what his name is. Guess we’ll never know.”

“We must name him, Dr. K.!” Rachel’s voice was adamant.

“Yes, child, you’re right,” agreed the doctor, “and I think that you deserve that honor. But remember, we are not equipped to meet this one’s needs, so his stay with us will be very short. I’ll have to make arrangements for his long-term care.”

Using the thin blanket, Korczak showed Rachel how to wrap the infant to preserve his body heat. She watched closely and tried to memorize the motions. But something about the blanket itself distracted her. It was worn, even threadbare in places, but a faint rabbit print was still noticeable. *The print! That’s it. One of the girls said that she gave a blanket with bunnies on it to a lady who had a newborn. This is the same baby!* The realization awed her.

“ . . . And that’s how to properly swaddle a newborn,” concluded the doctor. “See how calm he is now. He loves it.”

“Dr. K, you’re not going to believe this. Look closely at this blanket. It has rabbits on it. Do you remember one of the acts of kindness? It said that she gave a blanket with bunnies on it to a mother with a new baby. She said the mother and baby were living on the sidewalk by the old barbershop. That's where I found this baby."

The look on his face was a mixture of amazement and disbelief. He placed the bundle of boy in Rachel's arms then stood up. "Wait here in the office with him. I'll get Misha, and we'll see what she says. Stranger things have happened."

Rachel swayed from side to side as she cradled the dozing infant. She gazed at the tiny features on his face. Eyelashes as fine as spider's webbing fluttered slightly with the rhythm of sleep. A miniature mouth framed with tiny lips puckered occasionally in anticipation of warm milk. She was lost in wonder when Misha's words broke through her trance.

"Yes, sir, that's the blanket. Where's his mother?"

"She is no longer able to take care of him," answered the doctor.

Misha opened her mouth to ask another question then decided not to. She came over, sat on the bed next to Rachel, and caressed his head. "He likes my blanket, doesn't he?"

"Yes, Misha, he does," said Rachel. "And I'll bet that when he's asleep, he dreams of bunnies."

"Do you really think so?"

"I do."

"What's his name, Rachel?"

"Dr. K. and I were just talking about that before you came in. There is no way to know what his birth name was, so we must give him a name."

"Since Rachel saved his life, I think we should allow her to choose a name. What do you think?" The doctor picked Misha up and sat her on his knee.

"Oh yes, I agree." Misha turned and looked expectantly at Rachel.

"What about Isaac? He looks like an Isaac, and after all, it seems that God spared him. I had a brother once. He was—" Rachel cleared her throat and started again. "Stillborn. Mom and Dad named him Isaac. It was sad. The baby never felt the sun's warmth or heard the wind whistle. Never saw the clouds glide across the sky either. But this one will. This one will squint his eyes when he tries to look at the sun's face. He is going to learn to whistle like the wind and find pictures in the clouds. He will, Dr. K. He will!"

As he listened to Rachel's soulful words, he thanked God for every child in his care. For him, they were living, breathing wonders, sources of inspiration and fulfillment. He knew that without them, his life would be a barren wasteland, void of hope and vitality. The sound of a closing door broke the serenity of the moment, and the baby stirred and rooted against Rachel's chest.

"Looks like Isaac is hungry again. Potato stock is not as filling as a mother's milk. Better check his wrappings while I heat more."

"Can I help, Rachel? Please, I'll be careful," pleaded Misha.

"Certainly, but watch out. It might get messy."

The next couple of days were exhausting for Rachel. Isaac required round-the-clock attention. Luckily, Avram managed to find extra potatoes for the stock. Using a glass ear dropper to feed him was laborious, but Rachel didn't mind. She could see a little more color return to his cheeks after each feeding.

The clean-up part of the routine was the greatest challenge. Several times, Rachel got a warm shower before she could get his vital parts covered!

The moments she loved the most were those between wake and sleep. As he was drifting off, she would whisper words of hope in his ear. An indescribable joy, like healing rain, had just begun to wash away Rachel's sorrow when the time came.

"This might be easier for you if you let one of the others make this trip." Korczak's expression was full of concern. "My friends in the Underground have everything worked out. False identification papers have been secured. A childless couple is anxiously awaiting Isaac's arrival. The papers will identify him as a Christian, but the couple has vowed to tell him about his Jewish heritage."

"Please, Dr. K. This is something I have to do. I must deliver him into safe hands. I'm the one that the guard is paid to ignore. If he sees someone else, the arrangement could be ruined. There is too much at stake to risk it."

"I don't like it, but you are probably right. Now, how long has it been since his last feeding?"

"About fifteen minutes. He's content right now," answered Rachel.

"Then it is time for the sleeping medicine. Four drops should do the trick."

Isaac screwed up his face as the bitter drops were given, but within minutes, he sank into a deep sleep. Stefa helped Rachel as she wrapped the precious parcel and packed him into the potato sack. As a safety measure, a layer of his soiled wrappings was placed on top of him. If she were stopped, the wrappings would ensure that nosy guards kept their distance.

An uncomfortable quiet brooded in her corner of the ghetto as she headed for the meeting place. Though fraught with worry, she controlled her pace and expressions. Everything went as planned until she crossed at the first intersection of ghetto streets.

"Halte!" roared the guard.

Rachel stopped and froze. Something was out of place. There had never been a guard at this particular intersection. A wave of fear assaulted her before the guard ever came within striking distance. *I am a butterfly,* she thought, and breathed deeply. *I will float above my fear.* Her muscles relaxed, and reluctantly, she released the bag at her feet. She had avoided clutching it to her chest, and that was good. If she appeared the least bit protective of her cargo, the mission would be ruined.

"Where are you going?" he barked. "Curfew will be enforced in thirty minutes."

"I'm on an errand for my mom," answered Rachel, the calm tone in her voice belying her fear. She picked up the bag and swung it over her shoulder. To her relief, the bag remained still.

"What is in that sack?" The guard was young, and he was working hard to sound authoritative.

"My brother is sick. My mother thinks he might have typhus, so she asked me to take his soiled clothes to the dump." In order to appear convincing, she pulled the bag around and started to open it.

"Nein!" he ordered and stepped back. "I do not need to see or smell Jewish filth. Go about your nasty business, but you had better be out of sight before eight, or I will personally see that you are punished."

"Yes, sir." Rachel turned and walked away, holding her breath. When she was certain he was out of sight, she stopped and exhaled. Her pounding heart felt as if it would burst through the wall of her chest. She cradled the sack then ducked into a dark corner of an abandoned store to check on Isaac. She untied the clumsy knot at the end of the sack and reached inside to feel for his breathing. It was deep and steady. Whispering a prayer of thanks, she retied the knot, left the store, and resumed her journey.

It was seven forty-five when she reached the dump. The unexpected encounter with the new guard left no time for a thoughtful parting. She gently wedged the sack between two chunks of concrete and walked away from the sweetest source of joy she had ever known.

Two loyal resistance workers loaded pile after pile of rubbish in their garbage truck. They heard the girl wander into the dump, but they ignored her. The guard nearest the dump heard her as well, but he fingered the wad of money in his pocket and strolled in the opposite direction. This payment included an extra incentive that would more than cover the cost of his daughter's recent medical bills. The extra would buy her the dollhouse she'd been wanting. Taking bribe money from Jews was risky business, but he was certain the look on his daughter's face when he brought home the dollhouse would be worth it.

The garbage truck creaked and groaned under its load as one of the workers slipped into the cab with a tiny bundle.

Court Is in Session

The week before Hanukkah should have been brimming with anticipation and excitement. Plans were underway for another festive celebration. One group of children was rehearsing a holiday play written by Korczak. Others were making candleholders or menorahs and presents for one another. The gathering room hummed with activity.

Rachel sat next to Korczak. He had appointed her assistant director, and thus far, the job had demanded little effort. For that, she was thankful. The cast members were eager and were directing themselves. Consequently, the doctor was able to focus on his distracted and troubled assistant.

"I miss the savvy and willful Rachel. Where is she?" Korczak's eyes were full of concern.

"I've always loved Hanukkah, Dr. K., but these days, I feel ... " She paused and searched for the right word. Isaac was gone. His absence was eating away at the small reserve of hope within her. She missed Avram too. It had been two weeks since he'd left the orphanage and joined the forced-labor group, so the

extra measure of security he provided was not there.
" ... empty," Rachel finished. "I feel empty."

"I see. Emptiness, a condition of the heart as well as the stomach. It seems that these days we must work equally hard to fill both. I do have good news from my Underground friends. Little Isaac has gained four pounds and has started to smile. His new parents wanted you to have this." Korczak reached into his coat pocket, pulled out a folded piece of paper, and gave it to Rachel. She unfolded the letter and read aloud.

> *Rachel,*
>
> *Words cannot express the gratitude we feel for your act of heroism. It was a precious gift that has brought joy to many lives. When you and Isaac crossed paths that night, you made a selfless choice. He was weak and helpless. Given your own desperation, I can imagine how difficult it must have been to ignore your needs to save his life. Because of your sacrifice, Isaac has a future. And we promise to do everything within our power to make sure he grows into a fine young man. He will hear the story of how a courageous, young Jewish girl named Rachel saved him. It will be such a grand story that he will ask to hear it again and again.*
>
> *Rachel, we're confident that one day, the horrible nightmare you are living will end. And when it does, please know that you have a home with us. We will welcome you with open arms, just as we did Isaac.*
>
> *May our heartfelt words bring you hope,*
> *Your grateful Gentile friends*

Rachel folded the letter and tucked it into her coat pocket. "Will this nightmare ever end, Dr. K.?"

"It has to, Rachel. It has to," he repeated, trying to convince himself as well. "Now, my dear, it's time for dinner and baths. Won't a hot, soapy bath be nice?" he asked.

"We have soap? It's been two months since we've had soap for bathing. How did you get it?"

"I barged into President Czerniakow's office this morning and told him that I wouldn't leave until the Jewish council gave me a three-month supply of soap for bathing and coal for heating our bath water. He told me that it would take at least a week to gather the supplies. Thinking that I would be satisfied, he went right back to his busy work. So I sat down, pulled out my book, and started reading. The poor man tried his best to ignore me, but after twenty minutes, he was quite uncomfortable." There was a spark of mischief in Korczak's eyes as he told the story.

"So what did he do when he realized you weren't going to leave?" asked Rachel.

"He left the office and made the necessary contacts. Thirty minutes later, I was loading the supplies on the cart." As he spoke, the spark in his eyes burst into a rebellious flame.

"I bet he dreads your visits almost as much as visits from the German commandant he answers to," commented Rachel.

"Yes, he is truly caught in the middle. He must answer to his own people as well as the Germans. I would not want to be in his yarmulke. The token salary he receives does not make up for the pain caused by the ulcers eating away at his stomach," he replied.

The call to dinner brought rehearsal to an end.

Rachel and Korczak walked arm in arm into the kitchen and helped with the last minute preparations. Korczak lined the three- and four-year-olds up at the washbasin while Rachel helped Stefa dish up dinner. A slice of bread, thin potato soup, and raisins made up the evening's fare. Stefa told the children that the raisins were a special treat from Avram. It was a feasible fib. Avram had been gone for two weeks, and it would be easy for him to stop by any day on his way home from work. Rachel hoped he would soon.

Soap or no soap, the second and fourth Friday evenings were bath nights. A huge galvanized washtub that doubled as a storage container was emptied of its books and toys and moved near the fireplace. Water was heated and poured into the tub. Since water was a precious commodity, it was never wasted. Half a tub was used for bathing all the girls. When the last round of girls finished, it was dumped and filled a second time for the boys.

Rachel, Hannah, and Elizabeth always helped Stefa bathe the youngest ones. It was an enjoyable task. Their innocence and lack of inhibitions often provided unexpected entertainment.

"Sister, when will mine get as big as yours?" Sarah was sitting cross-legged in the tub with her head leaned back and her eyes closed. "When will I get to wear one of those breasty things?"

Giggles erupted and flooded the room as Rachel

rinsed the soap from the little girl's long, dark curls. "When the time comes for you to have a boyfriend, yours will be just the right size," answered Rachel.

"But I already have a boyfriend," claimed Sarah. "Avram is my boyfriend, remember?"

"I suppose there are different kinds of boyfriends, Sarah. When you have a boyfriend the same age as you are, one that you want to kiss, then your chest will be noticeable." Rachel smiled as she remembered asking her mom the same questions.

Stefa chimed in, "And that better be awhile, little one. Now, out you go. Dry off and go stand next to the fire. Elizabeth will help you with your hair."

A pot of boiling water was added to the tub before the next three girls stepped in. This group vowed never to have boyfriends.

"Boys are icky!" commented one.

"They smell funny too. I would never kiss a stinky boy!" claimed another.

"You'll change your mind about that in a few years," promised Stefa.

Nine- and ten-year-old girls didn't need help with bathing, so Rachel sat by the fire and soaked in the warmth. She was listening to their plans for their first dates when she spotted the peeper.

Rachel saw the tip of Moishi's nose and his dark eyes as they peered at the budding bathers. She stood up in a leisurely manner, intent on catching the rascal. Mingling amongst the chattering girls, she inched her way out of his line of sight. When she reached the entryway, she jumped around the corner and grabbed a handful of his unruly hair.

"Aaagghh!" hollered Moishi.

"Just what do you think you're doing, you villain? How dare you spy on us! Did you get your eyes and ears full?" barked Rachel as she tightened her grip on the clump of hair.

"Please don't hurt me, Rachel," Moishi begged. "I haven't been here long. Honest."

"I'm not going to hurt you, but I am going to take you to Dr. K., and you're going to tell him what you were doing." She let go of his hair, took him by the arm, and dragged him to the doctor's office.

Korczak was weighing the boys and recording the information when the two appeared at the door.

Rachel let go of his arm and pushed him forward. "Dr. K., Moishi has something to tell you." He turned back to see if Rachel was going to hang around for the confession. When he realized that she wasn't going anywhere, he knew he had to be truthful.

"Rachel caught me spying," he admitted.

"Tell him who you were spying on," Rachel prodded.

"I was spying on some of the girls."

Rachel lost her patience with the boy. She grabbed his ear and twisted, "Tell him what they were doing, Moishi. Tell him! Stop trying to weasel your way out of telling the whole truth."

"Oh, get off my back. I was just listening to their silly conversations." Moishi plopped down on the bed and leaned against the wall.

"You were too busy looking to do any listening!

Those girls were bathing, and you got an eyeful!" roared Rachel.

Korczak broke his silence. "Moishi, Moishi. What were you thinking?" He gave the offender a few seconds to feel the gravity of what he had done. "On second thought, don't answer that question. I don't think I want to know what you were thinking. Moishi, what you did is very serious. You have offended many people." He turned his attention to Rachel and announced, "This is a matter that must be settled in court." His words hung in the air like menacing clouds.

Rachel left the doctor's office while Moishi continued to plead for mercy. She returned to the bathing area and was bombarded with questions. "Who was that hollering in the hallway?"

"What happened?"

"Where did you go?"

She explained what had happened while she waited for her turn in the tub. Her listeners were indignant.

"The nerve of him," snapped Miriam, her cheeks flushed with anger. "His sinful eyes should be taped shut for a week. That would teach him a lesson." The other girls nodded in agreement.

"He will be justly punished. The judges will see to that," commented Stefa. "Okay, you three are the last ones. I've added some hot water, so you'll want to get in while it's still warm."

Rachel stripped and joined Hannah and Elizabeth in the tub. At first, the older girls had felt awkward bathing together, but not for long. A bath was a luxury to be appreciated, even in the absence of privacy. The gritty soap smelled stale, but it did wash away the layers of grime. Grime from the streets. Grime from the dump. Grime from traveling through the sewage tunnels. And grime from the grime.

Just as the girls were about to tackle their hair, Stefa surprised them by pulling out a bottle of shampoo. All three girls squealed with delight.

"Oh my gosh! This is unbelievable. How did you get it?"

Hannah squeezed a small amount into her hand. "It smells like budding roses on a spring morning."

"I found it in one of the packages delivered by our Underground friends. It's time that we write them a thank-you note. Would you three take care of that for me?" asked Stefa. "Give it to Dr. K. when it is finished. He will give it to his contact, and that person will see that it gets into the hands of one of the Underground leaders."

The bath and the shampoo did wonders for Rachel's spirits. Their lighter moods made it difficult for them to fall asleep, so Hannah, Elizabeth, and Rachel took turns brushing one another's hair and telling stories. With each stroke of the brush, the fresh scent of rose petals cleansed the air.

When she finally did lie down, she drifted into a curious dream. A sword and horse had just been presented to Lady Rachel, the first female in the kingdom to be dubbed knight. The horse, a chain of roses around his neck, carried the lady through the pressing crowd.

It was Saturday, and court was in session. The panel of judges was comprised of three boys and three girls. Elizabeth had been chosen as one of the girls. Each judge listened intently as Rachel told her story.

"I was sitting by the fireplace waiting for my turn to bathe when I noticed Moishi was peeking around the side of the entryway." Rachel pointed to Chana, Luisa, and Miriam and continued. "He was watching these girls as they bathed. I slowly made my way around the room. He was so focused on their bare bodies that he didn't even notice me. I reached around and grabbed him by the hair. He squalled like a noisy peacock and begged me not to hurt him. He promised he hadn't been there long, but how can we know that? Who knows how long he had been standing there or how much longer he would have spied on us if I hadn't caught him? Anyway, I let go of his hair and took him by the arm to Dr. K.'s office. I told the doctor what happened and then returned to the bathing area." Rachel sat down and waited for the cross-examination.

Moishi had asked for an advocate to represent him, and Dr. K. had assigned Rubin, a twelve-year-old, to the case. Rachel watched him as he stood and pulled a piece of paper from his pocket. *At least he combed his hair for the occasion.*

Rubin cleared his throat and asked his first question. "Rachel, when did Chana, Miriam, and Luisa realize that Moishi was spying on them?"

"None of the girls knew what happened until

after I returned from Dr. K.'s office. I handled it the way I did to avoid more trouble. Some of the girls in the room would have hunted him down and pinched the stuffing out of him had they known." Rachel turned and glared at Moishi. "You better be glad that I saved your senseless hide."

At the last comment, Rubin addressed the panel. "Judges, would you please tell the prosecution that insulting the defendant is not allowed."

Joshua, the lead judge, responded, "He's right on that point, Rachel. Your comments should be based on what actually happened, not on what could have happened."

Korczak sat in the back, taking in every word. He noted Joshua's clear and sensible judgment and smiled. For years, Korczak had been trying to convince adults that children deserved more credit than they were given. He firmly believed that with gentle guidance, children could govern themselves.

Rubin continued, "As Rachel stated, she was the only one who knew he was spying until after she returned from the doctor's office. The three victims did not know that they were being watched. If Rachel had kept the matter between her and Moishi, we would have all been spared the extra trouble. The defense asks that the judges consider this when deciding on a consequence."

"And what if one of the girls had been your sister, Rubin? Would you still have the same opinion?" Rachel turned to the judges and proclaimed, "There are more than three victims here. When this peeper violated the privacy of three girls, he offended every female in this home." Rachel's voice was filled with conviction.

"Now that's stretching it, Rachel. Why must females exaggerate so? My father always said that a woman can stretch a story to the point of absurdity. And as you can see, judges, that is just what Rachel has done. She has turned a harmless little prank into a seemingly violent crime."

Anger blazed in Rachel's eyes as she rounded on Rubin. "There's a fool in every house, as *my* father use to say. Judges, it appears that Rubin feels the need to attack women in general in order to defend his client, and that is a sure sign of a weak defense. Let's put an end to this foolishness and proceed."

Joshua turned to Rubin and asked, "Is your client prepared to make a statement before this court goes into recess, or does the defense rest?"

Before Rubin could answer, Moishi popped up and declared, "Judges, Rachel makes me look like a pervert, but I'm not. Honest. My own grandfather was caught peeking in my grandmother's window once when she was changing. And she still married him! I'm a curious boy with a deep appreciation for females. Is that such a crime?"

"Tell me, Moishi. What is it about a female that earns your deep appreciation? Is it her character or her curves?" snapped Rachel. This last question drew gasps from many of the children. The girls saw Rachel as a noble and worthy representative; the boys saw a lioness, cunning and relentless.

The judges whispered among themselves and then quieted so Joshua could make his announcement. "We have heard both sides, and the panel is ready to deliberate. Court is adjourned and will resume in one hour."

Korczak encouraged the children to practice the Hanukkah songs while they waited for the verdict. He reminded them that the holiday event was only two weeks away. "People will pay to see the program, so we must give them their money's worth."

Feeling lighter in spirit, Rachel joined in the singing. The words were timeless.

> Who can retell the things that befell us?
> Who can count them?
> In every age, a hero or sage came to our aid!

As their voices blended, an uncanny feeling overwhelmed Rachel. The song stirred something deep within her. Powerful images, buried in the depths of her mind, were resurrected.

The throne room was magnificent. Every feature was touched with gold. But Moses wasn't interested in gold. He was there on a mission for his people. Standing before the powerful pharaoh, Ramses, he demanded, "Let my people go!"

Rachel blinked and the scene was gone, replaced by a familiar but haunting image.

A crowd was gathered around the broken streetcar listening to the man's passionate speech. "Look beneath your fear and find the simmering anger.

Harness it, and rise up as one against the enemy." Then in mid-sentence, her father collapsed.

Rachel covered her eyes with her hands, and the image was shrouded by thick fog. Mere seconds passed before the scene changed.

A stunning white horse with a chain of roses around his neck stepped out of the fog. Atop his back sat a valiant knight. Her face was marked with a bold beauty. Deep, dark eyes revealed her courage and determination. She smiled knowingly at the entourage cheering her on. Their pain was her pain; their suffering, her suffering.

This last image seemed familiar. She was trying to make sense of the scene when the end of the song broke through her reverie.

> Hark! In days of yore, in Israel's ancient land,
> Brave Maccabeus led the faithful band.
> But now all Israel must as one arise,
> Redeem itself thru deed and sacrifice.

This song is not just about the past. It speaks of the present and a future, and somehow I'm going to be a part of it.

"Rachel. Rachel," Stefa repeated. "Come and sit down. We are waiting on you. Joshua is ready to deliver the sentence. You can continue your daydream later."

Rachel rejoined the group just as Joshua stood to read the verdict.

"This panel of judges has ruled. Moishi Joskowicz, you are guilty of invading the privacy of females who were bathing and dressing. We believe that it was your natural curiosity, not evil intent, that led you to do such a thing. Nevertheless, your violation of their privacy was inappropriate and demeaning. Moishi, there is much more to a person than physical appearance. Traits such as intelligence, honesty, diligence, humor, and kindness are a truer reflection of one's character. You must learn to look beyond a female's physical appearance in order to truly determine what kind of person she is. Therefore, in addition to your public apology, you are to identify one positive trait for every female in our home. When you have identified the traits, you must write one compliment based on that trait for each of them. Be prepared to deliver the compliments two weeks from today."

Applause from every female and a handful of the males filled the room. Rachel looked at Moishi and snickered. The boy's face was frozen in disbelief.

Dr. Korczak made his way to the front of the room, a proud smile adorning his face. "I am very impressed with this panel of judges. Their thoughtful deliberation has produced what I believe to be a fitting sentence." He turned to the defendant and said, "Moishi, you will present your apology tomorrow after breakfast. Remember that you must explain why you are sorry in order for the apology to be complete." Moishi groaned an acknowledgement and shook his head. "Now, let us return to our preparation and practice. Hanukkah comes!"

Rumors

The executions shattered the lightened mood that had settled in the ghetto. Seventeen smugglers. Seventeen lifelines that had thwarted the enemy's plan. Seventeen heroes, martyred to the Nazi war machine.

When she heard the news, Rachel was swept into a violent storm of emotion. Until now, she'd been able to bury much of her fear in the depths of her mind. Not anymore. Every layer of her consciousness was flooded with terror. *That could have been Joshua. That could have been Hannah or Elizabeth. That could have been me. We could have been lined up against the killing wall. Our blood—*

"Rachel. Rachel!" repeated Dr. K. "Are you okay? You look pale. Let's go to my office. I want to give you a quick checkup."

"I'm fine, Dr. K. I'm just tired. I'm sorry I didn't answer you. I've been doing a lot of daydreaming."

"I did quite a lot of that when I was your age, but it didn't make me pale. Come. I insist on a checkup."

Rachel followed him to his office. It smelled of alcohol, cough syrup, and futility. He motioned for her to sit on the bed while he rummaged through the clutter on his desk.

"Let's check your weight first." Korczak opened a tablet and searched for Rachel's record. "Two weeks ago you weighed ninety-four pounds. What does the scale say today?"

"It says eighty-eight pounds."

Korczak shook his head and whispered something under his breath. "Sit down and let me listen to your lungs and heart."

He placed the cold ear of the stethoscope on her back and listened. Then he moved it to her upper chest. "The lungs are clear, and your heart is strong."

He finished by checking her eyes, ears, and reflexes.

"See, I'm fine, Dr. K. You worry too much."

Korczak backed the chair up and studied her for a moment. He opened his mouth to say something then stopped. He closed the tablet, stood, and walked to his desk. While his back was turned, he said, "Rachel, you know that you are at the age when girls begin ... " He paused and finished, "If you have any questions about female development, please see Stefa."

"Yes, Dr. K. I will." She got up and started to leave, her cheeks flushed with embarrassment.

"Oh, Rachel, I almost forgot. From now on, you and Elizabeth are not to make any more visits to the dump."

"But we need those deliveries, Dr. K. The dump is inside the ghetto, and the guard is paid to keep quiet. There is little danger."

"Yes, Rachel, the supplies are valuable, but recent events have jeopardized the current arrangement. Don't fret. The Underground is a clever operation. The flow of supplies will continue. And by the way," he remarked as she left the room, "it's my job to worry about you."

The bi-weekly trip to the dump had become an adventure she would miss, but at the same time, Rachel felt relieved. She had already decided not to risk sneaking out of the ghetto again until the visions of bloody corpses, each wearing her face, disappeared.

The first day of Hanukkah fell on December 15, 1941. Rumors of America's entry into the war had finally reached the ghetto. Hope was resurrected once again, and people looked forward to the eight-day celebration with eager hearts. That afternoon, Korczak asked the oldest ones to supervise the last-minute holiday preparations for a short time while he and a couple of his staff members ran an errand. Rachel watched as the actors and actresses polished their performances.

The children rehearsed the last scene of the play. Joshua played the part of the Shammash, the ninth candle on the menorah. He had to light the other candles, played by eight smaller children. A paper flame, attached to Josh's head with a headband, was his simple costume. The eight children were lined up, four and four, with a small space in between. As the Shammash, the taller candle, Joshua stood here.

On cue, he left his place to light the other candles. He bent over slightly and touched his flame to the top of each child's head. Then flames, identical to Josh's, were released from their hiding places inside the headbands. While he lit the candles, a brother and sister were in the forefront quarreling with one another. The Shammash, saddened by the bickering, stopped and turned to the unruly siblings. "Do not quarrel, children. There is already too much conflict in the world. One must begin the path to peace within one's own home. After that, the time will come when peace will prevail everywhere in the world." The scene ended with the nine burning candles and the siblings singing.

Who can retell the things that befell us?
Who can count them?
In every age, a hero or sage came to our aid!
Hark! In days of yore, in Israel's ancient land,
Brave Maccabeus led the faithful band.
But now all Israel must as one arise,
Redeem itself thru deed and sacrifice.

As the cast members dispersed, Rachel made her way over to her friend. "Pretty good for such a slippery fellow!"

"You flatter me, my lady. Tell me more," Joshua begged.

"Absolutely not! You tell me. Who gave you lessons in charm? Your mom or your dad?"

"I learned from the best, my dad." A hint of sadness crept into his jade-colored eyes.

Sensing his sorrow, Rachel changed the subject.

"Have you seen or heard from Avram? He's been gone for almost a month now. Looks like he forgot his way home."

"Rumor has it, my dear Rachel, that Avram will be here this very evening to help with the program. Of course, we all know the real reason for his visit."

"We do?" asked Rachel, her eyebrows lifted. "And what is that?"

"Drop the pretense, Rachel. He is coming to see you."

"This play has your imagination working overtime. Avram and I are friends, nothing more."

"Sure," replied Josh. "Whatever you say."

Just as Rachel opened her mouth to protest, she heard an unnerving sound. It wasn't a scream, a volley of gunfire, or a despondent cry. It wasn't the thunderous bark of a guard. It was the sound of silence. She and Josh exchanged anxious looks as they made their way back to the gathering room. There, a wondrous sight met their eyes.

Everyone had assembled around a brass menorah as tall as Sarah. Its stunning beauty arrested the moment and cheered the hopeless spirits. Small packages, one for each child, lay beneath the polished ornament.

Among the gifts was another beautiful sight. Little treasures, vibrant with color. Round, edible jewels. Oranges. Small and insignificant in times of plenty but priceless in the eyes of the frail children.

Josh and Rachel joined the silent throng and listened as Korczak spoke. "Children, today is the first day of Hanukkah. At sundown, we will light the first candle and present our program. It is my prayer that our presentation will bring hope to the hearts of those who come. If we are to inspire others, hope must be alive within us. This menorah and the gifts beneath it were delivered by our Christian allies. Let us close our eyes and offer a prayer of thanksgiving for friends and for the gift of hope."

Hope. It slips in and out of my life like shadows. It's—

Sarah's muffled squeal interrupted Rachel's thoughts. When she reached for the child's hand, someone took hers. A sideways glance revealed the cause for Sarah's outburst; Avram had slipped into the crowd and scooped Sarah up into his arms.

His hand felt calloused yet warm and tender. Rachel smiled at the gesture, and without realizing it, she snuggled into Avram's side. All too soon, though, the prayerful moment ended. Their hands parted as their eyes met. He winked at Rachel and turned to Sarah. "Tell me, little one, am I still your boyfriend, or have you replaced me?"

"No, I haven't found anyone else. I tried to, but no one would wink at me. I've been practicing, though. Watch." Sarah turned Avram's head so she had his full attention, screwed up the corner of her mouth, and winked hard at him.

"Well, look at you! You're ready to take on the world." Avram's eyes smiled as he soaked in the child's adoration.

"Yes," said Sarah proudly. "You learned me to wink good. I winked at Doctor Papa yesterday, and he smiled real big."

"I'm glad I learned you something. Winking is an important skill. I couldn't get along without it. Hey, those oranges are disappearing fast. Run over there, please, ma'am, and grab one for yourself and Rachel."

Sarah sprang from his arms and skipped over to the menorah. Stefa was busy putting gifts and oranges into eager hands.

He turned to Rachel. "What a bundle of energy! She's grown taller while I've been gone. Taller but thinner. You've lost more weight too. Are you okay? You look a bit pale." Avram's eyes revealed concern and admiration.

"First Dr. K, and now you. I feel fine. And who in this forsaken ghetto is not losing weight? Thank goodness for the deliveries from our friends in the Underground because I haven't been out of the ghetto since the executions."

"I'm glad to know that. And don't you risk it any time soon. The guards have been instructed to shoot smugglers on sight."

"They don't have to have instructions to shoot. Losing a bet. Running out of cigarettes. Catching a cold. They're all good reasons to kill a Jew." Rachel's words were laced with scorn. "The executions terrified me, and I retreated. But I won't stay put for long. I can't. Smuggling is my way to fight back."

"There are other ways. That's one reason for my visit this evening." His voice lowered to a whisper. "There are rumors of organized resistance right here in the ghetto."

"How do you know this?" asked Rachel, her voice barely audible.

"I overheard some men talking in the freight yard."

"What are your plans?" Rachel was thrilled that he was confiding in her.

"I intend to find out more about this group. If it does exist, I plan to join." Avram's resolve bled through his hushed tone.

"But you're just fifteen. Do you really think they'll let you participate?"

"According to rumor, there are kids as young as thirteen involved."

The conversation was interrupted when Sarah reappeared, her arms filled with oranges and gifts. "There was enough for you too, Avram."

"Sit down, Sarah, and I'll help you peel your orange." As Rachel broke the waxy peel, she noticed that the invigorating scent of citrus had permeated the room. She closed her eyes and took a deep breath. In an instant, the everyday smells of decaying garbage, dried blood, and terror were gone.

For a moment, just for a moment, the world was filled with intoxicating aromas: tiny orange peels and the sweet breath of a little girl.

"What heavenly smells!" Rachel exclaimed.

"Oranges were my mother's favorite fruit." A wistful look passed across Avram's face, but it didn't linger. Sarah's enthusiasm chased it away.

As Rachel peeled, Sarah's little fingers went to work. She carefully loosened and unfolded the brown paper on each end of the packages.

"Gloves!" squealed Sarah. "Now I won't get cramps in my fingers at night." She fit one pair onto her own hands and proceeded to fit a second pair onto Avram's long fingers. "Oh no!" she cried. "They don't fit you." Her gleeful expression changed to one of worry as she continued to coax the winter coverings onto his hands.

"It's okay, Sarah. Long fingers don't get as cold as little ones. I'll take them, though. I know someone who can use them." Like wind that chases away fog, Avram's words dispelled the worry lines that had appeared on Sarah's forehead.

"Okay, you two, eat up." Rachel distributed the orange slices, and the three of them sat in silence as they ate. Mealtime had become a sacred affair.

When all that remained of the oranges was the tantalizing scent, Sarah jumped up and announced, "I'm going to take these brown gift wrappings to Stefa. We can use them for our handwriting lessons." She bounded off, and once again, Avram and Rachel were alone.

"About this resistance group. Will you keep me informed?" whispered Rachel.

Avram moved so that he and Rachel were side by side rather than across from one another. "Yes. It will give me a reason to drop in more often. I've missed your company."

"What is the work like at the freight yard?" Rachel inched closer to his side and basked in his presence.

"Grueling, especially for the elderly men. They are made to carry unreasonably heavy loads. And if they stumble or fall, they are beaten. The overseers are vicious. They walk about with their sticks and guns, stalking us like hounds after a wounded fox."

"How do you manage it? I don't think I could."

Silence crept between the two of them, and Avram shrank into a quiet contemplation. The space between them became an icy chasm, swallowing up every shred of warmth that Rachel tried to convey.

"I pretend that I am a machine. Machines have no feelings. They perform without thinking. Then in the evening, I pray for forgiveness."

Rachel noticed that his lively brown eyes were strangely hollow. His knees were drawn into his chest, his arms wrapped tightly around them. "You do that to survive," she consoled.

"Yes, but when the overseers are beating the elderly men, I keep working. I turn a deaf ear to their cries. In those moments, there is no difference between the man and the machine."

Rachel brushed a tear from his cheek. "Except machines don't cry, Avram. Those men understand your position. The conditions we are made to live in force us to do the unthinkable. A couple of months ago, I stripped a dead man of his belongings without blinking an eye. Our instinct to survive has taken over. It's scary."

"Can we change the subject?" he asked. His arms relaxed their hold on his knees, and the chasm closed. "This is Hanukkah, a time for celebration." He shifted back toward Rachel and reached into his coat pocket. "Oh, and before I forget, I have something for you." He pulled out a small package. "It's nothing grand, but it's something I want you to have. They belonged to my mother."

Rachel unwrapped a pair of silver combs studded with tiny pearls. She gasped at their splendor. "Avram, they are more than grand. I've never owned anything this elegant."

"May I put them in?" he asked.

"Yes, I'd like that."

He knelt in front of her, and with a tenderness that surprised Rachel, he pinned them in her thick hair. Avram stepped back to admire her. They added grace to each feature: her rich brown eyes, high cheekbones, the perfectly symmetrical jaw line, and the dark brown freckle at the base of her right cheek. "They look every bit as beautiful on you as they did on my mother."

Just as she was about to express her gratitude, Dr. K. came over and interrupted. "Avram, our guests will be arriving any time now. In addition to their admission fee, each guest should give you a loaf of bread. Do not let them in unless they have both."

"Yes, sir. I'll see to it." He turned and headed for the table that had been placed by the door but not before casting Rachel a fond wink.

A Midnight Rendezvous

Korczak was a brilliant man. Beneath his desire to bring hope to the community lay an ulterior motive; the Hanukkah program was yet another opportunity to solicit sympathy for his orphaned children. The program achieved both goals. Gloomy spirits were lifted, and sympathy in the form of bills made its way into Korczak's wallet.

Eight days of small Hanukkah treats worked up a sweet magic. Bickering stopped, tummy aches disappeared, and contagious smiles replaced tearful frowns. By the time the last candle was lit, a tranquil glow radiated from the face of every child.

As Christmas approached, Rachel noticed that the guards seemed preoccupied. She took it as a sign that it was time. Time to return to the streets of Warsaw. Time to meet Avram. Time to resist. A fierce determination had replaced much of the terror that followed the executions. It was that determination that would see her through the difficult times ahead. She hoped she was ready.

It was early morning on the eve of Christmas when Rachel headed out the door, waste pail in hand. She set a brisk pace in an attempt to ward off the biting cold. Thoughts of Avram kept her company along the way: his charming smile and the touch of his fingers as they slipped lightly through hers. She blushed as she remembered the kiss on her cheek.

Maybe it was the lightness in her step or the smile on her face that bothered the guard. Perhaps he had reached for a cigarette and found the package empty, or maybe it was just because he was him. Whatever the reason, Rachel was his target.

"Stop, Jew!" he commanded.

Rachel stopped as she was told. As he and a fellow guard crossed the street, she surveyed her situation. The undertaker's assistants had started their morning rounds, loading corpses onto the death wagon. They worked mindlessly: stoop, lift, toss. Repeat. An elderly man resting on the sidewalk in front of the barbershop was twenty feet away. His eyes communicated the usual message: *I wish I could help you, but …*

A few younger adults headed here and there seemed to know a confrontation was imminent but kept to their own business, secretly glad they were not the targets. They allowed the wind to sweep their thoughts away from Rachel's trouble.

Then she heard the whisper.

"Courage."

She looked back at the old man, but he had gone back to sleep.

"Courage, my little knight."

The sound was above, below, behind, and in front of her all at the same time. She set the pail down as the guards stepped onto the sidewalk. The older guard moved aside as the younger one stepped forward. It was the same young guard who had stopped her when she had taken Isaac to the dump.

"Running a nasty errand again, I see," scoffed the guard as he looked at the pail. "Jewish filth toting Jewish filth. You are well suited for it."

The senior guard snickered.

Rachel clasped her trembling hands behind her back. Her heart raced, and her knees locked. She looked beyond the guard's face at the death wagon and wondered if they would be picking up her body soon.

The blonde-headed, blue-eyed young recruit slapped Rachel's right cheek with his black leather glove. "Look at me when I'm addressing you!"

Her eyes watered, but she refused to cry. The anger that simmered within her began to boil. *I could kick him where Father said to kick a male attacker.*

"Not now," whispered the voice. "Patience."

Rachel locked eyes with him; Jewish brown met German blue. Smoldering anger collided with a sea of hate. It was then that he noticed the combs.

"Where did you get these pretty things? Pearls do not belong on swine." He reached up and snatched one from her hair. "Lovely trinkets. After I boil them, they will make a nice Christmas gift for my girlfriend." As he ripped the other one from her hair, it caught in a tangle.

"I'll have both of them," he vowed. He took a knife from his pocket and pulled her hair 'til it was taut. Rachel held her head with her hands as he butchered. She cursed silently.

When he had his prize, he knocked her to the ground and snorted like a pig. Before he turned away, he spit on her cheek. The older one slapped his back approvingly, and they sauntered away laughing.

Morning waned, and the hustle and bustle of the ghetto increased. People walked around the trembling mound of flesh on the sidewalk. Humanity abandoned her. A smoky gray cat rubbed against Rachel's leg, pulling her out of the stormy ocean of grief. She sat up, wiped the moisture from her face with her scarf, and looked around. The old man was gone. The death wagon was gone. Death had passed her by, but despair remained.

The crowd on the street had grown, but no one seemed concerned about her. *What have we become?*

"Something less than you, little friend," she mused as she stroked the hungry feline.

Suddenly nauseated by the smell of stale urine, Rachel forced herself up. She made her way to the ravine and dumped the waste into the revolting sewage. Before leaving, she added the soured contents of her stomach to the mix.

On the way back to the orphanage, Rachel tried to redirect the cat, but he would not be turned away. He seemed intent on escorting her back to the orphanage. To Rachel's relief, the return trip was uneventful. She felt that another confrontation would send her tumbling into a pit of insanity. Her nerves were on fire. Every sensation was magnified; the slightest wind was a blast, a passing glance a glare, and the cat's caress a blow.

When she reached the back door, she paused, straightened her hair, and wiped her face. She tried to sneak in unnoticed, but her escort made that quite impossible. A swarm of little ones ran up, pressed around the cat, and smothered him with attention. Stefa, curious about the commotion, came to investigate. She took one look at Rachel and knew something was wrong. She reached for Rachel's hand, and the two of them went into Korczak's office.

"What happened, child?" asked Stefa as they sat down on the twin bed. The lines on the caregiver's forehead and under her eyes deepened as she looked at Rachel.

Fresh waves of tears streamed down her cheeks. "A guard stopped me, the same one who stopped me when I was taking Isaac to the dump. When he saw the combs Avram gave me, he tore them from my hair. He said, 'Pearls do not belong on swine.' I hate them, Stefa. I hate the Germans!"

Stefa wrapped her arms around Rachel. The warmth of her embrace, contrasted with the guard's calculated coldness, triggered more hot, bitter tears.

"Why, Stefa? Why?"

"There is no explanation for this evil, child. All we can do is help and comfort one another." Stefa gently rocked the child as tears made their way down her own cheeks.

"But no one was willing to help me. No one but the cat."

"Would you have done differently if it had been the old man in trouble? What would you have done? What could you have done? In desperate times, the instinct to survive rises above all other human instincts. Compassion is an afterthought. The people who refused to help you will ask God's forgiveness before the day is over." The caregiver believed this with all of her heart. To believe anything different would have left her hopeless.

Stefa's words reminded her of Avram's words. "At night, I ask for forgiveness." This, along with Stefa's compassion, made Rachel feel better.

"You, my dear, need something to eat and a nap. Wait right here while I find a snack and a drink."

Stefa returned with a damp rag, a piece of bread, and a cup of warm liquid. Rachel washed her face and nibbled slowly on the bread. The drink made her cough and sputter at first, but after a few more sips, she softened to the sweet, fiery taste. It generated warmth that spread from her throat down to her toes.

"What is this stuff?" asked Rachel. "I've never tasted anything quite like it."

"It's Dr. K's special prescription," answered Stefa. "He said that it will help you rest."

As Rachel sipped the last of the potion, she noticed that her lurching stomach had quieted and her trembling hands relaxed. She climbed into the bed, and Stefa tucked the thin blanket around her.

"Shalom, my child. Rest peacefully."

Rachel was groggy, but she was sure that she heard two distinct voices utter the blessing.

Rachel awoke to a quiet midnight. Afraid that she'd slept through her engagement, she jumped up. *No way to know what time it is. I hope I haven't missed it.* There was no need to put on her coat, scarf, or hat. Since September, it had been necessary to sleep in them. She stepped into her shoes and slipped out of the doctor's office.

Everything but her stomach was quiet, and she felt a bit wobbly. She decided to stop by the kitchen on her way out. She'd slept through supper and was glad to find the boiled potato and slice of bread that Stefa had set aside. She crouched in the corner of the kitchen and ate the starchy duo. Then she stood up slowly, testing her stability. *Much better.*

With the stealth of a hunted animal, she crept out the back door and melted into the night. A bitter wind whipped and wailed. It stung Rachel's cheeks but could not shake her resolve. She adjusted her scarf and pressed on. This was her first meeting, and she didn't want to be late.

As she passed the broken streetcar, she heard it again. "Courage, Rachel."

"Father?" She glanced at the top of the car and then chided herself. *That drink went to my head. It's the wind, silly. It's been blowing all day.* She walked around to the back of the car, leaned up against it, and waited. Waited and prayed.

“There is a time for everything; there is a time for all things under the sun: a time to be born and a time to die, a time to laugh and a time to cry, a time to dance and a time to mourn, a time to seek and a time to lose, a time to forget and a time to remember. This day, I remember my father, who enriched my life with his love and his courage. Amen.”

“Amen,” added a soft voice.

Rachel jumped, despite the familiar tone. “*Gotenyu!* Dear God! You scared me. Don’t ever do that again! Did you forget where we are?” she whispered.

Avram drew her close and kissed her forehead. “Forgive me, *gelibte!* I didn’t want to disturb your meditation. It was beautiful. You honor your father in so many ways.”

“I was afraid that I was late in getting here. The morning was dreadful, and Dr. K. prescribed a sleep tonic. Anyway, I am here, and I am ready.”

Avram could not see the hurt in her eyes, but he heard it in her voice and felt it in her trembling body. “Are you sure you’re up to this?”

“No, I’m not sure. I’m not sure about anything right now. We can talk about my feelings later, though. We have somewhere to be. Do they know I’m coming?” Rachel adjusted her coat and scarf as they left the streetcar.

“Yes, they are expecting you. I’ve told them a few things, but you will have to answer some questions. Don’t be nervous. Everyone is screened.”

As she and Avram crept silently through the empty street, Rachel wondered what it meant to be screened.

The Sweetness of God

January was a busy month for death's angel, the *malekhamoves.* Typhus swept through the ghetto, infecting thousands. There was no ram's blood to brush on the doorframe of the orphanage, but by some inexplicable miracle, the orphans were spared from the fatal disease.

Nevertheless, coughs and sore throats abounded. Each night, a line of ailing children waited for his or her turn to gargle with saltwater. Afterward, Stefa scurried around from mattress to mattress, applying vapor rub to chests. The tireless caregiver amazed Rachel. She cooked, cleaned, taught, nursed, entertained, and miraculously kept the ghetto out of the orphanage. The oldest orphans realized what the younger ones did not; they were the luckiest children in the ghetto.

The grays and browns of the Jewish Quarter were hidden beneath a layer of ice and snow that seemed as permanent as death itself. But that worked to Rachel's advantage. Winter was the smuggler's friend; SS guards were reluctant to venture from their posts, and if the weather was bad enough, they would even turn their heads and pretend not to see the scavengers. The last week of January, conditions were brutally perfect, so Rachel bundled up and confronted the cold as well as her fears.

As she headed for the trash cans at the back of the produce mart, she hoped for a smooth and profitable run. The monthly birthday celebration was just a few days away, and she wanted to contribute something special.

Wilted mustard greens and potato peelings, she thought as she rummaged through the bins. *And look at the potato left on these peelings. Stefa can add both of these to a pot of her infamous lucky soup.*

After concealing the goods in the liner of her overcoat, Rachel moved on.

The next two stops had already been plundered. No bits of spicy Polish sausage. No stale crackers or chunks of moldy cheese. No apple cores either. So Rachel rubbed some warmth back into her hands and headed to the Catholic church.

A bitter wind nipped at her nose and face as she dug through the compost pile. Tossing aside eggshells, banana peels, and pecan shells with her frozen fingers, she uncovered the burlap bundle. She secured it on the rope tied to her waist. Just as she was about to leave, she heard the sweet voice.

"Rachel. Come to the back door. Let me look at you."

She recognized the voice but dared not abandon caution altogether.

"Rachel, it's Sister Agnes. Come. I have something else for you."

Rachel was drawn to the nun's gentle voice. She ran to the door and fell into the arms of the plump woman. Words spilled from her mouth like water from a faucet. "Oh, Sister Agnes, it's so good to see you. Thank you for all the manna packages. There are 152 of us now, and we're always hungry. What is the news about the war? And where is God?"

Sister Agnes positioned Rachel at arm's length. From the light of the waning moon, she surveyed the child. "So thin. You must have lost twenty pounds." She drew Rachel back into her warm embrace. "God has no hand in this war, Rachel. It is man's doing. Man, with his insatiable appetite for power. Oh, child, I wish I could make things better."

"You've done all you can, Sister. Much more than we could expect." Rachel tried to sound reassuring.

"I'm not so sure about that. But I believe that a time is coming when I can do more. And when God reveals that opportunity, I will act. Now, I have something extra for you, but I'm afraid that it won't feed 152 of you." She placed a warm bundle in Rachel's hands. "Sweet potatoes. That was our meal tonight. We were reminded to look for the sweetness of God, even in the midst of this vile war." A pleasant smile replaced her anxious expression. "And here it is, right in front of me."

"Sister, you are so thoughtful. Kindness..." Rachel paused, deep in thought. "It doesn't exist in the ghetto anymore. People are too desperate. Jew will inform on Jew if it will buy him extra bread and potatoes. Sometimes I wonder—"

An owl's screech interrupted her and startled both of them. For Rachel, it was an alarm. She was reluctant to leave the nun's presence, but she knew she had to go. She gave the woman one last hug then left.

As the child walked away, Sister Agnes prayed, "Heavenly Father, God of the Jew and the Gentile, protect this child and keep her for your kingdom here on earth."

"Look at this bag of shelled peanuts! What a treat this will be!" exclaimed Stefa. "Where on earth did these come from? Do you know, Hannah?"

Hannah glanced at Rachel and then answered. "Maybe it came from one of the damaged packages Dr. K. collected from the post office. He made a trip yesterday." Rachel and the other smugglers had become quite adept at covering for each other.

Part of the explanation is true, thought Rachel. *He did make a trip to the post office. And he did return with packages but not one with peanuts. Thanks to Sister Agnes, that was my gift.* She smiled inwardly, proud of her efforts.

"Shall we save them for the birthday celebration tomorrow?" asked Stefa.

"Yes. They will make the perfect treat."

"Rachel, I saw Avram on my way back from the mill," said Stefa. "His birthday is on the last day of the month, so I invited him to the celebration. He was rather pleased."

Hannah nudged Rachel with her elbow and giggled.

"Now, you girls need to go about your business while I go about mine."

Anticipation

"Sister, sister, our boyfriend is here," cried Sarah. Blushing with embarrassment, Rachel turned to see Avram walking toward her with Sarah sitting on his shoulders.

"This sack of potatoes is awfully heavy. I think I'll unload and have a rest." Avram sat down, reached for the tiny tot's hands, and leaned back, laying her gently on the floor.

Sarah scrambled around to face him. "Again, Avram, again!"

"Tell you what, after lunch we'll play hide and seek. How about that?"

"Yippee. Will you play too, Rachel?"

"Absolutely. Now, why don't you go and see if lunch is ready. I'm hungry."

Sarah darted off, leaving the two of them to talk.

"Does she run everywhere she goes?" asked Avram.

"Yes, she does. I guess it helps her get rid of some of that extra energy. Dr. K. has cancelled all outside play because of the typhus epidemic."

Rachel motioned Avram toward the stairs. They sat on the bottom step and talked. "I saw Sister Agnes last night. She feels that there is something more she must do to help. She believes that God will reveal the opportunity when the time is right."

"Are you thinking what I'm thinking?" he asked.

"I bet I am. She's trustworthy and dependable."

"Yes, and since the church has been so quiet, they are not a target. You know, it just might work. She would be a valuable contact. Let's suggest it at Wednesday's meeting."

"Avram, can we go visit your aunt and uncle again? I have something I want to share with them." Anticipation danced in her eyes.

"Your eyes ..." He brushed her cheek with his hand. "They're exceptionally beautiful today." He blushed when he realized he had spoken his thoughts aloud. "Yes, I suppose we can visit them. But we'll have to get in a game of hide and seek before we go."

"Excuse me," said Elizabeth.

Rachel inched toward Avram to allow Elizabeth enough room to access the stairs. When she started to move back, Avram put his arm around her waist and said, "Others may need to use the stairs. Why don't you stay close."

The gesture pleased Rachel. Their fondness for one another was growing. His tenderness stirred something within Rachel, something she'd never felt before. The budding relationship had restored hope; she could even imagine a future with him.

The lunch bell rang for the older orphans. Avram stood, turned, and extended his hand to help her up.

Rachel thanked him with a smile that said things Avram longed to hear.

"Lucky soup with bread on the side. And after that, I have a surprise." Stefa's eyes beamed with excitement. She served each of the older orphans then left the room.

"Good ol' lucky soup," said Avram. "Sure do miss this place."

"Let's survey our luck." Joshua probed the contents of his bowl. "Horse meat, potato pieces with the peeling, onion, and something mushy and green. Looks like algae."

"It's not algae, silly." Rachel's voice became a whisper. "It's mustard greens. I found them in the garbage cans behind the produce mart."

"I brought Stefa the horse meat. I was lucky enough to be one of the first people on the scene," Joshua said proudly.

"I traded an Underground newspaper I found outside the ghetto for a bunch of wild onions," Hannah added.

"You read it first, didn't you? Was there news of the war?" Avram asked eagerly.

"One article reported on some big conference held in Germany. It said the purpose of the meeting was to secure Nazi plans for the future. I didn't understand all of what I read, but they supposedly discussed the 'Jewish problem.' One of the solutions discussed was something called *resettlement.* They've already relocated us once. What could be worse than this rat hole?"

A grave silence came over the group. Each had

learned from their ventures in and out of the ghetto that Nazi brutality was endless. There was always something worse.

Elizabeth broke the silence. "Was there any good news?"

Hannah perked up. "Yes, I was getting around to that. Another article said that America, France, and Great Britain are beginning to work together. They are discussing ways to defeat Hitler."

"We must believe that they will," said Joshua.

The others nodded in silent agreement. As they finished off their lucky soup, Rachel wondered if luck would influence her destiny.

During the remainder of the celebration, Rachel anticipated the moment she would reveal her surprise for Avram. She rehearsed the scene in her mind as she helped Stefa with dessert, the finale of the celebration. The orphans were thrilled; the word *dessert* had almost been deleted from their vocabularies.

When their age group was called, they lined up in an orderly fashion. Stefa gave every child a cookie, and Rachel counted out five peanuts for each. The sweet and salty dessert reminded Rachel of Sister Agnes's words: *Look for the sweetness of God in the midst of sorrow and suffering.*

The Sunday morning sun took a bite out of the frigid wind as Rachel and Avram walked hand in hand. Inside Rachel's coat was the "something extra" that Sister Agnes had given her. Avram had asked a dozen questions, trying to figure out the purpose of their visit to his aunt and uncle.

"What could Rachel, the queen of smugglers, have to share with my aunt and uncle? What did you find? Tell me," he implored.

"It would ruin the surprise. Now stop interrogating me, or I'll have to—"

Rachel's words and steps were cut short when Rubinstein appeared from around the corner of a building.

"Have you heard? Typhus strikes the rich and the poor, the high and the mighty, the good and the evil, the dogs, the cats, and the weevils. All are equal in the ghetto." After the absurd man's pronouncement, he skipped off and left the two of them in the wake of his laughter. This made the sixth or seventh time Rachel had encountered the zany jester, yet she was still appalled by his ghastly antics.

"Bless his poor mother," said Rachel and shook her head. "If she's alive, I bet she doesn't claim him. Who would?"

"I know, but you have to admit, there is some truth in his words."

"Yes, but most people can't see the truth for his madness." Rachel continued walking.

"I suppose those people will find it elsewhere," offered Avram.

"Well, we're almost there, and I'm excited. I've been thinking about this for two days now. Nothing can spoil this surprise. Not even that madman!"

"Aunt Giena, Uncle Samuel, it's me, Avram. And Rachel is with me. Can we come in?" The two waited patiently for the door to open.

"You say you are my nephew. So tell me, what was your mother's name?" The woman's voice was thick with suspicion.

Avram sighed and shook his head but replied respectfully. "My mother was your sister, Ruth."

When the door opened, Avram could only see Samuel. "Hello, my boy. Come in, come in." He extended his arm to welcome them. "Giena, it's all right, dear. Avram and his little friend have come to see us again."

The panic-stricken woman appeared from behind Samuel. No sooner were Avram and Rachel clear of the door than she hurriedly shut and bolted it then turned around, her back pressed against it. She sighed deeply and said, "Last night, we heard a terrible banging on the neighbors' door. Today, they are gone. The wolves got them, I tell you. See, the enemy comes to the door first. If they can't get in that way ..."

Suddenly, Giena's paranoia dissolved, and her demeanor changed. Like the sun that appears from behind a menacing cloud, her expression brightened. "Samuel, these sweet children have come to visit us again. Where shall we sit and talk?"

Rachel took the cue. "Can we sit at the table? I have something to share with everyone." She unbuttoned her coat as she walked to the table. The others followed, curious at what she was about to reveal. She placed the small package in the center of the table and announced, "There is a birthday to celebrate. Avram will be sixteen in just a few days. So let's eat this feast together." She unwrapped two plump sweet potatoes and stood back. Three gasps, followed by a delighted squeal, dispelled any remaining anxiety.

"Look at these beautiful potatoes! Where did you ... ? Oh my!" Giena's hands framed the look of surprise on her face.

Samuel spoke next. "I'm honored that you want to share with us."

"Rachel, this ... " Avram fumbled for the right words but gave up. He would thank her later, privately. "Let's have a knife to cut them."

Rachel handed each of them a half, then served herself. "Easier to cut them four ways than 152."

As they slowly savored each bite, Rachel quietly thanked Sister Agnes for sharing the sweetness of God.

United in Purpose

Their faces were gaunt, their bodies worn and weary, but their resolve was firm. Rachel surveyed the group of rebels: a chemist, a butcher, scholars, businessmen, students, a doctor, teenage boys and girls, young single women, Orthodox and Conservative Jews, the outspoken and the reserved. Different in countless ways but united in purpose. Resistance.

"The goal of tonight's meeting is to discuss possible contacts. If we are to accomplish anything, we must have assistance from the outside. It is imperative that we secure a steady flow of supplies, namely weapons. But we will also need bandages, medicines, non-perishable food, candles, and news. News in any form."

Zivia's eyes scanned the crowded bunker. "We are in the process of establishing a relay of contacts through the Polish Underground. But that is only a start. A river is fed by many streams."

Rachel admired the woman's self-assurance. Few knew it, but Zivia Lubetkin was the only female leader in the fighting organization. There was strength in her posture, conviction in her voice, and fire in her eyes. If there was any doubt about the woman's competence, it did not show in the faces of those present.

Avram shared the news from the paper Hannah had found. Disquieted murmurs rippled through the room at the mention of the word *resettlement.*

Zivia addressed the group. "What Avram says is true. A resettlement camp has been opened in Chelmno. A group of Jews from villages surrounding Chelmno was taken there. They were promised better living conditions, an abundance of food, and job opportunities. But according to a new source, those promises were lies used to get them to go willingly. Our source was part of the group. He escaped from the camp and fled to Warsaw. And he brought news. Disturbing news. According to his report, the people taken to the camp were murdered. We have no reason to believe that he is lying, but we are trying to verify his story."

Looks of despair darkened their sallow faces.

Then came the explosions. Explosions of anger. Righteous anger.

"They are the seeds of Satan, these Germans!"

"Vicious murderers!" cried another.

"We must avenge their deaths!"

Zivia jumped on a chair and held up her hand. "Brothers and sisters ... " The bitter cries gradually simmered—an answer to her appeal for silence. "We must not let our anger lead to premature action. Let us harness it and use it to our advantage." Then the hand that called for silence curled into a fist. "The time will come when the enemy's blood will stain the ghetto streets. Until that time, we must curb our anger in order to make sound plans."

"She is right," said a scholar. "Carelessness is often the result of unbridled anger."

Zivia sat down, but her shadow still loomed. "Now, if our dream of a successful revolt is to be realized, we must have contacts. Does anyone have any recommendations?"

A lanky, bearded man with the longest arms Rachel had ever seen stood and spoke. "My brother-in-law has a brother. He owns the bookstore next to the produce mart. It's close. He would be willing to help."

"Why?" asked Zivia. "He is not Jewish. Why would he be willing to risk his life?"

Without hesitation, the man replied. "The Nazis went through every book in his store. They confiscated over half of his stock and burned them. Two thousand "dangerous" titles were incinerated."

Rachel's mind had been at work as the man talked. She stood and made an offer. "That bookstore is on my route. I could pick up any packages and deliver them."

Zivia studied the girl. "I remember that your name is Rachel, but I cannot remember how old you are."

"I will be fourteen in April."

The chemist rose. "Should we put someone so young in this kind of danger?" He turned to Rachel. "Your parents—"

"Both dead," Rachel interrupted, her voice quivering. "Father because he openly tried to rally our people and get them to move beyond their fear. Mother—" She stopped and swallowed the knot in her throat. "Mother hanged herself because someone she worked with came down with typhus. She was afraid of infecting Father and me." Emboldened, Rachel continued. "I appreciate your concern, but I stare this kind of danger in the face every time I leave this place."

She turned back to Zivia and added, "One of my stops is the Catholic church. There is a nun who leaves packages of food for me. She buries them in the compost pile by the garden in the backyard of the building. A few nights ago, Sister Agnes told me that she is praying for additional opportunities to help."

Rachel sat down, afraid she had said too much. Avram took her hand and held it firmly. "That was brilliant," he whispered.

"Rachel, please tell us how long you've been smuggling goods into the ghetto."

Zivia knew the answer. The girl's screening and background check had provided the leader with sufficient evidence to trust in her ability. But she was wise enough to know that she had to build the teenager's credibility with the group.

"A year now."

"How long have you known this Sister Agnes?"

"As long as I can remember. My parents owned a nursery, and Sister Agnes was a regular customer. The nun tends the garden and the flower beds at the church."

"And how long has Sister Agnes been leaving packages for you?"

"As long as I've been smuggling. She calls them manna packages."

The line of questioning worked. Zivia read the expressions on the faces of the members and noted the consensus. "It seems that your Sister Agnes is a friend to the Jew as well as the Gentile. Ask her if she would be willing to visit with a member of the Polish Underground."

Millions of stars shone down on the chilly February night as two silent figures made their way down the ghetto street. They slipped in and out of dark recesses. They inched noiselessly past two talkative guards. One was boasting that his son had come of age and joined Hitler's Youth.

When they reached the back door to the orphan house on Sienna Street, Avram took Rachel's trembling hands and kissed them both. "You were amazing tonight," he whispered.

"I had no intention of saying that much, but once I started I couldn't stop."

"Will you see Sister Agnes before the next meeting?"

"I'll make my rounds again on Friday. I seldom see her, but I have a feeling that she is close by every time I'm there. I'll go to the back door and knock."

"Maybe Sister Agnes is God's way of watching over you." He drew her close and hugged her. "Thank her for me, will you?"

Rachel could have stood there in his arms all

night, but she knew that it was dangerous to stretch their luck too far. "You'd better be going," she said and stepped back. "Even the protection of the Sister Agneses of the world can't help us here."

Avram squeezed her hands, slid into the shadows, and disappeared as the crescent moon slipped behind a thin cloud.

Connections

This is David and Goliath all over again, thought Rachel as she neared the church. *And where is my stone?*

Thorns of doubt and fear pricked at her resolve. *I don't know what I was thinking when I volunteered for this. If I'm caught smuggling weapons, they'll know. They will torture me to get—*

"Look beneath your fear. Righteous anger is your weapon." The voice came and left with a single gust of wind.

Rachel knocked softly on the apartment door. She counted to ten and then spoke the password. "Hadassah, the beloved Queen Esther."

Zivia opened the door and replied, "May her courage live on in us." As soon as Rachel was inside, the leader shut and bolted the door. "I'm thankful for your safety. Come and sit at the table. I will make us a cup of lemonade."

"Lemonade?" Rachel was surprised. "Sugar? In the ghetto?"

"Sugar substitute," Zivia answered. "The chemist in our group makes it from vegetable remnants."

"And the lemon?"

Zivia joined Rachel at the table. She set a small bowl of sunflower seeds between them. "The lemon is from a dear friend of mine. A courier. Without her armband, she can acquire goods and information throughout Warsaw."

As Rachel sipped the lemonade, her taste buds were resurrected from their bland graves. "Please thank your clever friend for me. This is delightful. I'm curious, though. How is she able to get supplies so easily?"

"Her hair is light brown, and she speaks Polish fluently. Like you, she uses her talents and connections to help others. Speaking of talents, did tonight's venture run smoothly?"

Rachel took the precious package from beneath her coat, and when she laid it on the table, she felt like the weight of a thousand stars was lifted from her shoulders. "Yes. The streets were quiet. Too quiet. Rubinstein has been babbling about the calm before the storm. And people actually believe him! Maybe the quiet has something to do with Passover. People are waiting for the evil to pass. Whatever the reason, the stillness made me nervous, so I came back through the sewer. I think I'll return that way every time from now on."

Zivia picked up the package. "I'll be back in a moment. Help yourself to some sunflower seeds."

Rachel chewed slowly. *Eat in slow motion; nutrients that are consumed too quickly are useless.* The doctor's words marched through her mind every time she ate.

"Returning through the sewer is wise, especially when you are carrying a package for us." Zivia rejoined Rachel at the table.

"Can you tell me what's in the package?" Rachel asked, overcome with curiosity.

"You won't know what's in the packages. It's our way to protect you. Sister Agnes won't know. Sometimes it's best not to know."

"I understand," said Rachel. And she did. She'd heard the stories of the SS officers torturing Jews for information.

"The next package will be ready for pickup on Sunday. The back of the bookstore. Knock three times with a pause in between, then twice in succession. Tell the man who opens the door that you are there to pick up the writing tablets."

"Will the packages ever be too big for me to hide?"

"Never," promised Zivia. "Now, my friend, eat some more sunflower seeds and finish your lemonade while I clear the couch. You did tell your guardians that you would be staying the night with Avram's aunt and uncle, didn't you?"

"Yes, and they weren't the least bit suspicious," answered Rachel. "They want us to visit extended family members and close friends."

"There is a strong kinship among the members of our group. You will soon discover that we are a unique family. The unity we've built with each other makes our personal losses easier to bear."

"The orphanage is like that too. Dr. Korczak and Stefa are loving guardians. They both work hard to provide the best care possible for each of us."

"Your Dr. Korczak is an extraordinary man. His circle of influence includes Jews and Gentiles from every corner of Poland. The prominent Jews of the ghetto avoid him. Do you know what title they've given him?"

"No," said Rachel as she sat on the couch. "What is it?"

The corners of Zivia's mouth widened into a grin. "They call him the Ghetto Troll; he won't let them cross his path without a donation for his children."

Rachel smiled knowingly as Zivia left the room. She settled onto the couch for the night. *How true,* she thought. *And the wealthy are the billy goats.*

The Path of Defiance

Knock three times with a pause in between, then two times in succession. The silent recitation marched through her mind as she dug through the trash bins. She pocketed a single cabbage core, leaned against the wall, and scanned the area. Something wasn't right.

No rats, thought Rachel. *That's it. For two weeks now, I've not had to compete with rats. Guess hunger has swallowed them too.* She shuddered and moved on.

Ask the man who opens the door for the writing tablets. Rachel had rehearsed the instructions repeatedly. *No room for mistakes.* As she neared the bookstore, the urge to sneeze drove her into the nearest shop. Thanks to the bitter winter, she was able to slip right in; the wood used to board up Jewish businesses had been stripped and used for firewood. She felt her way to the back of the room and bumped into a counter. Ducking behind it, she covered her mouth and nose. The sneeze was nothing more than a squeak, but in her business, a squeak could be fatal.

Since I'm here, I might as well snoop around a bit.

She ran her hand along the back of the counter and discovered sliding doors that opened to an area that had once been encased by glass. Shards littered the inside of the case, each one a silent witness to Nazi tyranny. Underneath the encased area was a deep shelf. Rachel reached in and felt about. As she swept her hand across the floor of the cabinet, she was surprised to find a hole the size of a finger. Curiosity whispered in her ear. "Such a tidy little hole. Too perfect to be accidental. Bet the Germans missed it." She held her breath and stuck her right index finger in the hole. *It's a sliding panel,* thought Rachel, *meant to hide this nifty nook.*

Beneath the panel was a secret space, a space created by the owner of the jewelry store. He was a respected Jewish elder, skilled in his craft, and proud of the business that his family had sustained for three generations. It was that pride that had made him determined not to let the Germans take everything. After the first few Jewish businesses were confiscated, he took his most valuable diamonds, put them in a black velvet pouch, and tucked it into the hiding place.

Then the fateful night came. German trucks poured into Warsaw's business districts. The sound of shattered glass pierced the quiet night. Walls were branded with swastikas. Invaders plundered and desecrated their targets. But in their savage frenzy, clever corners were overlooked.

What if this is a trap? What if the bookstore owner made a deal with the Germans? Good intentions are often for-

gotten in desperate times. Rachel's mind quivered, but her hand was steady. She delivered the prescribed knock exactly as instructed. While she waited for the door to open, she fingered the velvety bundle in her pocket.

"Yes?" The cautious voice answered, but the door remained closed.

Rachel sighed with relief; the man's trepidation was a sign that all was well. "I'm here for the writing tablets."

The door opened to reveal a short man with wiry salt and pepper hair. He stared at Rachel in disbelief. "My brother told me it would be a child, but I didn't believe him." He handed her the package. "Wait a second. I've got something for you."

Rachel turned and searched the darkness. In the distance, she heard the low rumble of a truck. Closer, the scraping of a forlorn branch against a crippled building.

"The wife insisted that your courage be rewarded. Please take it." He handed her a hard-boiled egg and smiled. "Nothing pleases me more than to defy the Germans."

"Yes, sir. I know what you mean. It's scary, but satisfying all the same." Rachel tucked the package away and took the egg. "Thank you for your kindness. Resistance would be impossible without people like you." She turned to leave. "I should be going now. I'm sure I'll see you again soon."

The man watched in wonder as Rachel melted into the darkness. "Knights come in all sizes these days. There is hope for Poland yet."

Divided Loyalties

"Sister, will you help me write in my diary?" Sarah asked as she joined Rachel at one of the study tables.

"Sure." Rachel closed her own diary and set it aside. "Do you remember what month it is?"

"Yes, it's March, my birthday month."

"March the twentieth, 1942." Rachel spoke as she wrote. "Okay, how do you want to start this entry?"

"My birthday is eight days away. I hope the crawlies in my hair are gone by then. I don't want to spend my birthday scratching. Stefa says it will help if I let her cut my hair. I'm thinking about it. Devorah has the crawlies too, but she doesn't—"

"Slow down, Sarah. I can't keep up." Rachel recorded the thoughts word for word. "Devorah doesn't what?"

"She doesn't know she has them because she's visiting Princess Klu Klu's island in her sleep. She's been gone for two days. Dr. K. said she may not come back. I think she likes Princess Klu Klu more than she likes me. That makes me sad."

Rachel put the pencil down, turned, and cradled

Sarah in her arms. "Devorah loves both of you. And I'll bet that if she decides to stay, she'll set up a special hammock for you. Right next to hers."

"Do you really think so?" Twin embers of hope glowed in Sarah's eyes.

"I'm going to go to the art table so I can add a picture to my entry. I know just what kind of hammock I want."

Sarah's words were the answer to Rachel's indecision; she knew what she had to do. She opened her own diary and read what she had written before being interrupted.

> *These days are gloomy. Dr. K. is getting weaker. He doesn't have the strength to make all of his rounds, so I've been helping him. We've received so few donations. Even the wealthy are running out of resources.*
>
> *I'm worried about Devorah. She has had a high fever for a week and has been unconscious for two days now. Dr. K. says that her body has a better chance of fighting whatever is causing the fever if she is unconscious. But he also said she might not make it. She needs medicine, and there is no money.*
>
> *The seven diamonds I found on my way to the bookstore last night have forced me to think about my loyalties. Until now, there would have been no question about what to do; seven of these little gems could feed, clothe, and medicate us for six months. But I have a second family now, and I have pledged …*

I've pledged to help them make a stand. A stand against the German monsters who are responsible for every death in this ghetto. Whether the death is instant or slow, they are the ones controlling Devorah's fate, not

God. So the diamonds, like my loyalties these days, must be divided. Rachel added these decisive thoughts to the entry, left the study table, and looked for Korczak.

The doctor had lost faith in his country. He had lost faith in himself. And he had lost faith in prayer. But his faith in children was as strong as ever. He believed in their purity, their potential, and their resilience. Rachel watched in awe as the man, fighting his own exhaustion and failing health, sat and bathed Devorah's feverish face. To chase away the gloom, he whistled a lighthearted tune.

"Excuse me, Dr. K., may I come in?" Rachel stood at the door, the velvet pouch cupped in her hands.

"Yes, but not too close. She's very sick, and we must assume it's something contagious. You're not feeling sick, are you?" Korczak's deep, dark eyes scanned Rachel for signs of illness. He reached for his stethoscope and struggled to stand.

"No, Dr. K., I feel fine. Please sit back and relax." Rachel grabbed the chair next to his desk and sat down. "Are there any signs that she may be getting better?"

"No, I'm afraid not." A hint of helplessness bled into his voice. "She needs a sulfa drug. A month ago, I could have managed this. I could have secured the resources needed to get the medicine. I'm afraid my best sources are drying up."

"Not all of them," offered Rachel as she revealed the pouch in her hand. "An anonymous donor gave these to Avram and asked him to make sure that you got them." She reached across and put the treasure in his shaky hand.

He steadied his left hand on his leg and emptied the pouch. A tremendous gasp jolted his entire body. "Merciful Mother of Methuselah! Look at these rocks! Four of them! They were given to Avram, you say?"

"Yes, sir."

"Man or woman?" Korczak delicately fingered each gem.

"Sir?"

"Was the donor a man or woman?"

Without hesitation, Rachel gave him a plausible answer. "An elderly woman. She told Avram that she had lost all of her family."

"The Germans are like swarms of locusts; they invade, destroy, and leave emptiness in their wake."

"Do you ever dream of fighting back?" The question was a subtle confession.

"I dream of escape. Princess Klu Klu's island. Planet Ro. That is the beauty of being a writer. You can create your own escapes." Korczak's knowing eyes met hers. "But I was young once. I understand the desire to resist."

The penetrating gaze made Rachel uncomfortable, so she redirected the conversation. "Sarah believes Devorah is visiting Klu Klu's island in her sleep. She is afraid that Devorah likes Klu Klu more and will decide to stay."

"I see," said the doctor, rubbing his chin. "Sarah asked me if sick people dream when they sleep. I saw the question as the perfect opportunity to gently prepare her for the worst. I did tell her that Devorah might not return from her dreams. Is she distressed?"

"I reassured Sarah that Devorah likes them both. I told her that if Devorah decided to stay, she would make her a special hammock next to hers. That seemed to give her some hope. When I left her, she was at the art table, adding a picture of a hammock to her diary entry."

Korczak smiled warmly. "What a blessing you are, Rachel! To bestow hope is a rare and beautiful gift."

"But hope doesn't fill empty stomachs." She looked over at Devorah. "And it doesn't buy medicine."

"Ah! But diamonds do." Korczak stood and pocketed the pouch. "Four will sustain us for a couple of months. Give Avram my thanks and tell him to stop in more often. He should take more meals with us."

Devorah shifted restlessly and whimpered. The doctor turned back to his charge. "Rachel, would you please ask Stefa to come and sit with her? I need to make some contacts."

As Rachel turned, she heard Korczak whispering to Devorah. "Medicine is on the way, little one. So the hammocks will have to wait."

The Chosen

Passover arrived, and the Jews remembered. But the Angel of Death forgot. It forgot to pass over the Jewish ghetto in Warsaw. The *malekhamoves* stopped for the suicidal. It stopped for the diseased. And it accompanied a band of cold-hearted killers as they stalked their targets.

Rachel and Avram sat in the bitter silence that blanketed the crowded bunker. The news was surreal. In the dark of night, German soldiers and SS men had hunted down and slaughtered fifty-two men.

An enraged voice shattered the quiet. "Why?"

"The leadership is studying the list of victims. They do not believe this was a random act. Our enemy is calculated and methodical." Zivia paused as if to taste the words before she spoke them. "There was only one thing in common among the men; they were all educated. Yitzhak Zuckerman, one of our leaders, was on the list. He got word ahead of time and went into hiding."

"Maybe the Germans have discovered us. Is it possible that we have been betrayed by an informant?" The butcher's question was one that many had already asked themselves.

"An ugly thought, but one that must be considered. This tragedy calls for tighter security measures. We are searching for additional meeting places so that we aren't meeting at the same place every time. A clever fox has many holes."

"I do have good news." Zivia glanced at Rachel with smiling eyes. "The organization has come upon an unexpected treasure: three sizable diamonds. This turn of luck will enable us to purchase several guns and a few knives. And supplies are beginning to trickle in through our network of contacts.

"We are also communicating with other fighting squads. Plans for tunneling are underway. It will be slow and grueling work, but it's work that must be done. The tunnels will be vital for moving to and from the different sections of the ghetto. They will enable us to avoid detection and provide a safe means of retreat. Kazik will be in charge of the tunneling operations for our group. Please make yourself available to help if he calls on you.

"Before we depart, let us offer a prayer of remembrance for our fifty-two brothers who were taken from us." Zivia motioned for everyone to stand. Their voices and hearts were heavy with grief, but the prayer was just what was needed to rekindle their determination.

"May God remember the souls of our brothers who have gone to their eternal home. In loving testimony to their lives, we pledge charity to help perpetuate ideals important to them. Through such deeds and through prayer and memory are their souls bound up in the bond of life. May these moments of meditation link us more strongly with their memory. May they rest eternally in dignity and peace. Amen."

Better than Diamonds

As Avram escorted Rachel back to the orphanage, she told him about the diamonds. "I told Dr. K. that an anonymous donor gave them to you and asked you to make sure that he got them. Since you're staying for the Passover meal, he's sure to thank you."

"So you need my cooperation, do you?" A mischievous grin played on his face. "Is it worth a kiss from the loveliest girl in the ghetto?"

The mischief was contagious. "That depends," answered Rachel. She winked and returned the grin.

"On what?"

"On how convincing you can be."

Rachel and Avram slipped into the gathering room just as Korczak began the service. "And we recall that the vine, which is always pruned as nothing else that bears fruit, has every branch cut away, leaving an old gnarled stump. Yet in the spring, as do all living things, it grows again. Thus we learn from the vine that what appears to be death is not an ending, but a resting and a re-gathering of strength for a new beginning." The doctor's voice was weak; it lacked the energy that came from passionate belief.

As the Seder, the Passover service, continued, Rachel thought of the fifty-two men, the smugglers who had been executed, and the nameless corpses she had to step over every time she ventured out. *What is spring? I don't see it here; everything around me is wilting. I can't hear spring; my ears are full of the sounds of suffering. I can't smell spring, but I do smell fear and death. And I don't remember what it tastes like. I only remember bread and potatoes.*

The large gathering room could no longer hold all the children, so two services had been planned. Two modified services. Their situation did not allow them to follow the prescribed guidelines for observing the holiday.

"This is the bread of affliction, the poor bread which our ancestors ate in the land of Egypt. May all who are hungry come and share our matzoh; may all who struggle for freedom come and share our spirit." Stefa took the flat loaves of dark bread and passed them around.

When the loaf reached Sarah, she broke off a small piece and said, "I've never tasted poor bread." She studied the piece before she put it in her mouth. "Where's the 'fliction? I don't see anything."

Rachel thought a moment and then answered. "Affliction is suffering, and suffering is all around us. The ladies that work at the secret mills have suffered. Sometimes their tears fall into the dough as they are making the bread. You can't see the affliction in the bread, but it's there."

"This leafy herb is on the table to remind us of the hyssop used by the Israelites as a brush to apply the blood of the Passover lamb to the doorframes of their homes. The saltwater represents the tears our ancestors shed while in slavery and the tears we shed each day for those around the world who are still oppressed. Come now, one row at a time, and dip a piece of parsley in the saltwater. After you eat it, you may take a drink from your canteens."

The shortened service ended with a Passover song. And then the feast began. Each child enjoyed a boiled egg, a piece of roasted meat, and a serving of charoset, a dish made with chopped apples and nuts, cinnamon, and grape juice. Rachel and Avram took their plates and sat on the bottom stair. They ate slowly, savoring each precious bite.

Korczak, leaning heavily on his cane, made his way through the maze of children. He looked at the two teenagers and for a moment saw a trace of hope.

"Avram, my boy, it's good to see you again."

"It's good to be here ... instead of out there. This place is a sanctuary. You and Stefa shielded me from the harsh reality for as long as you could. Thank you."

"Stefa is a fine assistant. I find myself relying on her more and more." He leaned against the wall and sighed. "It takes the strength and support of many to tend this place. The diamonds came at a critical time. See Devorah there? The one playing with Sarah? She is skipping about these days because of those diamonds. Thank you, son, for seeing to their delivery."

He started to hobble away then turned back. “And if you see the lady who donated them, give her my deepest thanks.”

Avram dug something out of his pocket and turned to Rachel. “Since I’m supposed to thank the woman who donated them, this can be a thank you and a birthday gift. I hope that tomorrow is a sweet day.”

Rachel untied the string, and the small cloth bundle fell open to reveal five Hershey’s kisses. Before she could stop herself, she pressed her hands on his face and kissed him. Her cheeks blushed, her lips buzzed, and her heart bubbled over all at once. “These are better than diamonds! Where on earth did you get them?”

“I’ve a candy man in the family, remember?” Avram peeled the foil away from one of the kisses and popped it into her mouth. “I agree with you, Rachel. Kisses are better than diamonds!”

Dark Rooms

May arrived, and the orphans searched for spring. What they found was lingering cold. It was too cold to put away their coats. Too cold to welcome the rain. And too cold for caterpillars.

"Sister, what is a butterfly?" Sarah squirmed in Rachel's lap as the tangles were combed from her hair.

"A butterfly?" The question stirred the pit of grief that bubbled within Rachel. She realized the Germans had robbed them of more than their material possessions. So much more. "A butterfly starts out as a caterpillar, a little worm." She remembered a time when she had let one inch its way up her leg. "It stores up energy by eating, and when it's full, it spins a cocoon—a safe, dark room—around itself and goes to sleep. Its body goes through many changes while it sleeps. When it wakes, it uses its colorful new wings to fly from the cocoon." She remembered the awe from witnessing such a miraculous rebirth once. After the butterfly took flight, her mother gently pulled the empty cocoon from the stem it was attached to. It made an exquisite show-and-tell item in first grade. "A butterfly is a delicate and beautiful creation, Sarah. Just like you."

"The orphanage is like a cocoon, isn't it, Rachel? It's dark because Dr. K. boarded up the windows. And I think it's a safe place. I hear terrible noises outside sometimes that frighten me. I've never heard those noises in here."

"Yes, Sarah, you're right. Our home is a haven. Dr. K. and Stefa work hard to keep us safe. And one day, those scary noises will stop. I promise."

Sarah popped up, flapped her arms, and fluttered off. "Then we will stretch our wings and fly out into a lovely new world."

This room was dark. *But not safe.* Naked female bodies pressed tightly against one another. The hot, thin air was saturated with the smells of body odor, uncertainty, and raw fear. Strangers embraced. Rachel watched as the armed guard threw small, naked figures on top of the standing crowd. When the room could hold no more, he shut the door and locked it. The sobs became screams. She tried to cover her ears, but her arms wouldn't move. She tried to close her eyes, but her vision remained fixed. She wasn't in the room but was just as helpless. As the screams of the dying subsided, her own scream was unleashed.

"She's feverish. Elizabeth, get me a damp cloth and a bowl of water." Stefa's tone was low but steady. She didn't want to wake the smaller girls across the room. "Rachel, can you hear me?"

The familiar voice was comforting. She wanted to answer, but she couldn't get the words to move. *I must be lying on the surface of the sun. I'm so hot ...*

The caregiver bathed Rachel's face, neck, and arms. She squeezed drops of cool water into her mouth while she rebuked the *malekhamoves.* "You will not satisfy your hunger here. Move on. This one is full of life. She is a fighter. Like every child in my care, she has a purpose to fulfill, and you will not interfere!"

The dark angel's presence hovered above Rachel's sleeping mat and waited for the bond between spirit and body to dissolve. But as dawn approached, the angel sensed its defeat; the will of the child, the will of her caregiver, and the presence of hope created an impenetrable barrier. It bowed to its victor and left.

"Can I come and sit by Rachel, Miss Stefa?" Sarah's plea was irresistible.

"Yes, it's safe now. The fever has left. I will have Elizabeth come and sit with her too. Let Rachel know when she wakes up that she is to stay in bed today, no matter how restless she gets. Will you do that for me?"

"Yes, ma'am. And don't you worry. I'll sit on her if she tries to get up."

The exhausted woman managed a smile before turning to leave. "I'll have your breakfast delivered."

Rachel opened her eyes and ran a hand through her damp hair. She looked for the guard but found Sarah instead. Overcome with sweet relief, she smiled into the face that hovered over hers. "Sarah, what are you doing here?"

"Miss Stefa assigned me to this very spot. Elizabeth too. You were sick, sick, sick with a fever all night." Feeling her newfound authority, Sarah continued. "We're supposed to make sure you stay in bed today. Do you understand, sister?"

"Dr. K. gave you some of the same medicine he gave Devorah, and Stefa was at your side all night long," explained Elizabeth.

"All I remember is the nightmare. A crowd of women ... in a dark room. Little girls ... the door closing—"

Sarah interrupted, her face aglow. "Were they in a cocoon? Did they grow colorful wings while they were asleep?"

Sarah's questions stunned Rachel. She stared at nothing and thought about everything: the picture of the butterfly she painted when she was five, the bruises on her lifeless mother's neck, delivering Isaac to the dump, joining the resistance, finding the diamonds, kissing Avram, and the unforeseeable future.

Sarah waved her hand in front of Rachel's eyes. "Well, did they? Did they fly away when the door was opened?"

Rachel turned her head away from Sarah. "I don't remember." Her voice trembled with an uncertainty that resembled dread. "The dream ended before the door was opened."

A look of dismay passed across Sarah's face. But it did not linger. It was quickly replaced with an inspirational glow. "You can finish the dream tonight and tell me all about it tomorrow. I want to color a picture of those butterflies."

Sensing Rachel's discomfort, Elizabeth made a suggestion. "I'm awfully hungry, Sarah. Will you go see about our breakfast?"

Sarah got up and skipped out of the room. Elizabeth took her place at Rachel's side. "That little one makes me tired. Where does she get her energy?"

"From her imagination." Rachel's answer was an afterthought. But it was just what she needed to put the troubling dream to rest. "The same place our dreams come from. Dark rooms, slaughtered caterpillars, and monsters—all inventions of the imagination."

Sarah returned, carrying a plate with their breakfast. Hannah was behind her with four cups of water. "We have jam with our bread this morning," Sarah announced. "Let's pretend that the water is tea and have a tea party."

The three older girls indulged their whimsical little companion. Each sipped tea from an ornate ceramic cup, nibbled on her bread, and described in detail the colors and designs on her delicate wings.

Voices

The room was small and plain. In one corner sat a desk, positioned near the only window, a small portal that looked out onto gray streets and dirty buildings. Inside the bottom drawer, the package waited. On top, books rested between a pair of bronzed praying hands. An oil lamp illuminated the pages of the book the woman cherished most. The one she thumbed through daily.

A bed made for one lined the opposite wall. The pillow lay unused on the floor. Although the Lenten season had officially ended two months earlier, she refused to afford herself the luxury of a pillow. *My Jewish brothers and sisters have been stripped of everything. Many sleep on sidewalks. Foxes have holes and birds have nests, but the Son of Man has no place to lay his head. Sleep I must, but I will not sleep in comfort.*

Sister Agnes knelt on the floor, her elbows on the bed, palms together in prayer. "Our Father, who art in heaven. Hallowed be thy name. Thy kingdom come. *Merciful God, replace this hellish kingdom the Nazis are building with your own.* Thy will be done. *These mon-*

sters have placed their will above yours. On earth as it is in heaven. Give us this day our daily bread. *Your people are starving. Young ones cry out in hunger. Older children risk their lives smuggling food into the ghettos.* And forgive us our trespasses. *Soon there will be blood on my hands. This I confess. The packages I relay. I do not see the contents, but I know. I am contributing to violence. Forgive me.* As we forgive those who—"

A familiar tapping interrupted her. The nun struggled to her feet. Her knees creaked in protest to the formal prayer session. She steadied herself with the help of the bed and walked over to the desk. Package in hand, she left the room.

"Did you find the carrots, child? Come here and let me give you a squeeze." Tears slid from the woman's sea-green eyes as she hugged Rachel.

"Carrots will make a nice addition to Miss Stefa's lucky soup." Rachel wiped away a tear that had wedged itself between worry lines. "Please don't fret, Sister. Avram is right; you are God's way of watching over me."

"I dreamed about you last night. You were alone and had no place to go. If you ever find yourself in that position, you know that you can come here, don't you?"

"I would never put you in that kind of—" The sound of heavy boots startled both of them into silence.

"Into the broom closet!" whispered Agnes, a note of panic in her voice. She shut the closet door just as the second visitor knocked softly on the back door. "Who is it?" Her heart thumped with fright.

"Someone who seeks sanctuary." A thick German accent confirmed her fear.

"You are a German soldier. How can I trust that you mean me no harm?"

"Woman, if my intent was to harm you, I would have knocked the door down. Please, Sister, honor your vows and let me in!" The voice was grave and insistent.

Sister Agnes had learned not to trust the Germans. "Acts of mercy and generosity," she said to herself. "Even to the wolf in sheep's clothing?" Her eyes glanced heavenward as she mumbled the question.

The man hurried through the door. Before closing it, he checked again to make sure he hadn't been followed. Then he bolted the door, turned, and sighed heavily.

Sister Agnes positioned her lamp so she could see his eyes. *Are they really the windows to the soul?* she wondered. Residual bruising and swelling surrounded both of them. She probed their depths. *They have the look of one who is haunted.*

"Thank you for your kindness, Sister." His blue eyes looked past her and scanned the hallway. "Where is the priest? I must confess." His voice faltered. "I ... I cannot go on like this."

Rachel listened intently from inside the closet.

"There is no one here who has the authority to hear your confession." Bitterness punctuated her words as she moved to open the door. "Our priest was arrested by your comrades."

"You don't understand, woman! I cannot leave this place until they stop searching for me. If they find me, they'll kill me."

The nun's hand was on the knob, and the soldier's hand pressed hard against the door. His wild eyes were fixed on his only hope. "I cannot kill another child!"

Perhaps he is desperate, broken, and penitent. More sheep than wolf. Agnes looked into his eyes again, searching for the truth.

And forgive those who trespass against us.

Don't you believe him for one minute! In the darkness of the closet, Rachel silently mouthed the words. She was reaching for the package inside her coat when she heard the unthinkable.

"Sanctuary is granted. Come with me, and I will take you to Mother Superior. She will explain the conditions of your stay and find a place for you to rest."

Rachel knew that Sister Agnes had cleared the way for a safe exit, but she was paralyzed by disbelief. *How can she protect a vicious Nazi killing machine? I don't—*

"Now is not the time. Don't try to make sense of her actions, Rachel. Leave!" the voice prodded.

In the confines of the small closet, Rachel realized where the voice was coming from. *It doesn't come from the wind. It's not the voice of a ghost. And it's not a symptom of insanity. It's real, and it comes from within me. My memories of Father, his ideals, and his teachings have given birth to it. It has been with me since his death, and it will be with me always.*

Rachel stepped out of the closet and looked down the long, empty hallway. The area was still clear, so she suspended her confusion and quietly left the church, still pondering the significance of the voice.

Never Enough

Rachel was three blocks from Zivia's apartment, the forbidden cargo safely tucked away in her coat, when it happened. The incident at the church had left her shaken but unusually alert. And that's what saved her from walking right into the dreadful scene.

The smell of gunpowder and blood, carried by the June wind, was the first sign that something was wrong. Terribly wrong. Rachel ducked into the broken streetcar and scrambled under a bench when she heard the raiders advance. Then a horrific concert of sounds tore through the night: boots slamming into doors, piercing screams, cracking bones, wailing mothers, children sobbing.

And gunshots.

The shots sent spasms of shock through Rachel, and her body jerked involuntarily with each one. She rammed her forehead into one of the iron bench legs as she curled into a fetal position. Seconds later, warm blood dripped from her temple. She reached into her coat for her scarf but pulled out the package instead.

The group of raiders was following orders. They were on one of the countless missions designed to save the Fatherland from ethnic impurity. Certain groups posed a threat to the evolution of Germany's super race. Their orders were simple; eliminate the threat. This ideology was so ingrained in the mind of the German soldiers that they killed their targets without an inkling of remorse. They proudly walked away from a slaughter with looks of pure satisfaction on their faces.

Rachel unwrapped the package. The soldiers had passed the streetcar, but the nightmare was not over. There were more targets to flush out. They were still close enough for her to hear the shots and the death cries. *Close enough for me to kill,* thought Rachel as she wrapped her hand around the pistol.

She crawled out from under the bench, knelt by a window, and peered out. The raiders were kicking in doors at an apartment building one block up from the streetcar. A small group of soldiers waited outside to receive the frightened victims.

The pistol felt strangely cold in her hand. She fumbled with the chamber, feeling like she did when she had tried to tie her shoe for the first time. When the bullets were in place, she closed it and took aim.

"You are too far away for a handgun," said the voice.

The nightmare began to repeat itself as women and children were chased from the building. Waiting soldiers caught them, threw them to the ground, and began kicking them.

"Then I must move closer," answered Rachel and got to her feet.

"Fire the gun and you will put the resistance in jeopardy." The voice was urgent.

Rachel tried to listen with her head, but the despair and agony of the screams clawed at her heart. "But they are innocent!"

"You are a victim too. A victim with limitations. You are outnumbered. You've never fired a gun. Reckless action will only endanger the mission to which you have committed."

Rachel cried as she unloaded the pistol and rewrapped it. She tucked her legs into her chest and rocked until the sounds of terror were swallowed up in the distance.

"You did the right thing, Rachel." Zivia tried to reassure her.

"I want to believe that." Rachel flinched as Zivia cleaned the cut on her forehead. "But their screams are still ringing in my ears."

"The time will come when the Germans will be the target. Then we will watch them run. We grow stronger each day."

As the woman put away the first aid supplies, Rachel thought of the maze of bodies she had walked through to get to the leader's apartment—bodies still warm from the last breath of life. She had somehow found the strength to stop at each one and close any eyelids that were fixed open.

"The *malekhamoves* is never satisfied," she said to the hungry roach that scurried across the floor. Her voice trembled, and her body shuddered.

Zivia returned, placed a cup on the table, and sat next to Rachel. "Please drink this. It will calm you and help you sleep."

Rachel sipped the liquid, and for a moment, her expression lightened. "Sweet and fiery, like the tonic Dr. Korczak made for me once."

"Let's go to the living room. I've got your bed ready."

Rachel settled onto the couch, drink in hand. "I hope it's strong enough to drive away nightmares."

"My father's recipe. Trust me; it will repel the worst of nightmares." Zivia sat by Rachel and continued. "He was a builder. Built houses. He understood that it took different people with different skills to complete a house. During the course of a project, each person arrived when he was needed, completed his part, then left. None of his comrades took on jobs outside of his area of expertise. Can you see how that ensured his success?"

"Yes, but you're not just talking about building houses, are you?" Rachel knew the answer before asking the question.

"Your contribution to our group is vital." Zivia took Rachel's hand, looked into her eyes, and continued, "And we are blessed to have you among us. But there will come a time when you will be needed elsewhere. Can you understand that?" She held Rachel's gaze and waited for an answer.

Rachel yawned, feeling warm and groggy. "I think so. But I do want to see the Germans run. That's a dream I wouldn't mind having," she whispered as her eyes closed.

Later as Zivia lay in her own bed, she pondered the fate of the resistance. *It will be ants against elephants, a grim battle with no hope of victory. And yet ants are worthy creatures. They are little but extremely wise. They are creatures of small stature, yet they store up their food in the summer. If we allow our collective wisdom to guide us, the Germans will soon know the power of Jewish honor!*

A Light on the Other Side of the Dark

"Why did you choose such a gloomy play? Both of Amal's parents have died, and he is on the verge of death himself. He even gives all of his toys away because he knows that death is coming for him." Rachel pushed another chair into place then stopped and looked expectantly at the doctor.

The old man paused, winded and weary. "Children need to know what Amal realizes toward the end of his sickness; there is a light on the other side of the dark, a healing light that will make them whole once more."

"You don't think we're going to survive this war, do you?" she asked incredulously.

Korczak stared past Rachel. "Hope is a fickle friend these days; sometimes she rises with the sun and soothes my aching bones, but at other times she leaves me to suffer, with no regard for my pain." He chuckled. "I don't make any sense, do I? Forgive me for my ramblings. I haven't been sleeping well."

I must speak to Stefa about him. He is not himself. "Do you remember telling Jakob that knights would rise up to save Poland's Jews?" Rachel resumed her task of putting chairs in place for the late-afternoon performance.

"Did I say that?" With considerable effort, he stood up and helped her.

"Yes, sir, you did. Jakob believed you, and so did I. There *are* knights Dr. K., right here in this ghetto. I dream about them. They are preparing for battle. We mustn't lose hope."

That evening, Rachel watched as Jakob played the part of Amal. *He is a natural. And look at the audience. They are spellbound.*

"I can see all the stars now, twinkling from the other side of dark." Jakob gazed out the window. The boards of one of them had been temporarily removed for the performance.

Joshua played the part of the royal physician, and Rubin played the part of Amal's uncle. As Sudha, the flower girl, Rachel had made her first appearance. While she waited for her part in the last scene, she cupped a single flower gently in both hands and breathed in the fresh scent of summer.

In the final scene, Amal has closed his eyes for the last time. The royal physician is at his side when Sudha arrives.

"When will he be awake?"

"Directly the King comes and calls him."

"Will you whisper a word for me in his ear?"

"What shall I say?"

"Tell him Sudha has not forgotten him."

A profound silence followed the last line of the play. For a second, the world that was and the world that was to come merged. As the moments ticked by, a smattering of applause erupted around the room.

Stefa introduced the actors and actresses to their audience as the children formed a receiving line. Warm handshakes and smiles were exchanged.

Avram was last in line. He took her hand, and the two of them quietly made their way to the stairs. They sat down together, leaving plenty of room for people to pass.

"May I?" he asked and reached for the white carnation. He placed it in her hair, the stem behind her right ear. "You grace the flower."

"It won't live long now that it has been cut." Sadness pooled in her eyes. "I hate it that things have to die."

Avram caressed her cheek with his hand. "What's wrong?"

"Where shall I begin? This play ... I have not enjoyed it at all. I'm glad it's over. I asked Dr. K. why he chose such a sad play, and he said, 'Children need to know that there is a light beyond the dark.' I'm afraid he's lost hope.

"And then there's Sister Agnes ... She has granted sanctuary to a German soldier. Can you believe it? Said something about her vows, acts of mercy, and forgiveness. I thought about discussing Sister Agnes with Zivia but decided not to. It would've felt like I was betraying her. And I couldn't do that ... not after all she's done for us.

"Zivia said something that bothered me too. She said that there would come a time when I would be needed elsewhere ... suggesting that I would leave the group. Nothing seems right, Avram. I'm so confused." She rested her head on his shoulder and sighed.

A few minutes of tender silence passed while Avram gathered his thoughts. "When someone we care deeply for loses hope, I believe that we can hope *for* them. You and I have a reason to be hopeful. We can't explain why, but we can reserve some of that hope for the doctor. Does that make sense?" He lifted her head and searched her eyes for understanding.

Rachel nodded, then nestled against his chest.

"And when a loyal friend does something we don't understand, I suppose we have to trust them. It's hard to imagine how Sister Agnes can be merciful to the enemy. But she has never betrayed you. And vows made to God are binding. We of all people know that."

"A remorseful German. Do you think it's possible, Avram?"

"I don't know. War seems so unpredictable. I imagine it must be very hard for Zivia and the other leaders to prepare for the unknown. Maybe that's why she said what she did. For everyone's sake, she feels that she has to remain open to different options. We must try to trust her too." Avram kissed her temple, held her tighter, and whispered words of hope in her ear.

She was getting drowsy when he began to stir. He rubbed her arms and asked, "Did you get the message about a change in plans? The next several meetings will be held at a bunker on Mila Street."

Rachel saw a group of girls walking toward the stairs and reluctantly pulled away from his comforting embrace. "Yes, Zivia told me," she said quietly. "I am to start making my deliveries there. She said one of her neighbors started to ask questions."

Avram yawned and squeezed her hand. "I'd love to hang around, but there are tunnels to dig. Tell me if my nose starts twitching involuntarily. I feel as if I'm turning into a mole."

Rachel smiled, and the last traces of her gloom evaporated. She wiped a smudge of dirt from his nose. "I knew you probably couldn't stay for dinner, so I packed you a little something for later." She handed him a small package. "If it's stale, just sprinkle a little dirt on it. That should spice it up."

"Until Thursday," he said and opened the door. "Be safe. Be alert. And remember to—" He was hushed with a soft, sweet kiss.

"No need to fuss so. I know what I'm doing." She winked fondly at him as she let go of his hand.

His eyes sparkled with surprise and pleasure. "Yes, I believe you do."

Gone

Rachel walked home under a gray, gloomy sky. Ominous clouds, heavy with rain, sagged and grumbled with sinister thunder. She took little notice of Mother Nature's threats, for they were mild compared to the German SS force. Her thoughts centered on the recent news and warnings given at the meeting.

The deportations had begun. On July 22, Korczak's birthday, Adam Czerniakow, president of the Jewish Council, had received official word. The council was ordered to assist German SS troops in rounding up Jews for resettlement in the east. Czerniakow did not cooperate. Worn and weary from the stress of mediating and managing, the broken man had taken his own life.

It was no loss for Rachel; she had hated the man. In her mind, any Jew who worked for the Germans was a traitor. And yet he had always managed to come through with extra supplies for Korczak's children. *Maybe he has finally found peace,* thought Rachel as she rounded a corner.

Zivia warned that deportations were taking

place daily, despite the Jewish Council's refusal to help. She told them that SS soldiers would lure Jews out of hiding with a promise of food. When they emerged, the armed men would surround them and force them to walk to the *Umschlagplatz,* the concentration point. Then they were herded into cattle cars and taken by railroad to a camp called Treblinka.

As she mused over the disturbing news, her pace quickened. *I must find a way to warn Korczak and Stefa without making them suspicious. But how? If they find out about my involvement with the resistance ...* Heavy raindrops interrupted her anxious thoughts. She stopped and looked up. The clouds were raining bitter tears upon the ghetto streets. Thunder boomed, and streaks of ghostly light flashed across the darkening sky. The August sun had gone into hiding.

A sense of dread crept up on Rachel and engulfed her. She rounded the last corner and broke into a run. When she reached the door, she stopped and tried to shake the rain and the gloom from her body. It was useless. She opened the door and was greeted by a haunting silence.

No singing. No crying. No arguing. An eerie absence of sound. As she walked into the gathering room, she knew something was terribly wrong. Children's belongings lay scattered across the floor like forgotten memories: a brush, a scarf, a tattered doll whose eyes were permanently closed, and Sarah's silkie. Rachel stooped down, picked up the silky remnant, and cried out. "Stefa! Dr. K!"

No answer.

In the kitchen, dirty breakfast plates and cups were still on the table.

"Sarah! Elizabeth! Hannah!" She ran up the steps two at a time. The second-floor sleeping area was littered with possessions too. It appeared everyone had left in a hurry.

She bolted down the stairs. "Joshua! Moishi! Rubin! Where are you?" Stopping at the foot of the stairs, she listened, desperate for an answer. The only sounds she heard were echoes.

"Why must we leave, Stefa?"

"Where are we going?"

"Why do they have guns, Dr. K.?"

"Sister's not here. Where is she? We can't leave without her."

Panic overwhelmed her. She crumbled to the floor, her heart pounding against the wall of her chest. Her head sank into her arms and knees. She struggled to breathe. Fear completely possessed her. Fear for the little ones, fear for the doctor, fear for the entire world.

When she looked up, she noticed that the door to the broom closet was cracked. *The hideout! That's where they are.* A wave of relief steadied her, and she got up and walked over to the closet. She opened the door, removed the waste pail, and lifted the burlap rug. Underneath it, on top of the trap door, lay a piece of folded paper with her name on it. She sank down against the wall and stared at it.

Drowning.

Rachel was drowning in dread. The kind of dread that comes from knowing, yet not wanting to know. She tried to reach for the paper, but her arms wouldn't move.

Countless minutes passed.

Then she heard the voices; voices arguing in German. The back door rattled and triggered her adrenaline. In one swift move, she grabbed the paper, dumped the contents of the waste pail, and shut the closet door. She was crouched in a dark corner of the bunker when she heard the voices again.

"We need to make sure we got every one of the little piglets," barked one. "There were almost two hundred of them. Check that closet. Someone could be hiding in there."

The younger one looked disdainfully at the excrement on the floor. "*Es gibt scheiBe auf dem fuBoden. JudescheiBe.* Can't you smell it? I'm not walking through that. Check it yourself. I'll look upstairs."

Silent tears streamed down Rachel's cheeks as she sat alone in the darkness. *What was I thinking? This hideout has been too small for all of us for months now.* Her body trembled from the sobs she suppressed, and within minutes, a violent case of the hiccups assailed her. To mute the sound, she grabbed the silkie, wadded it up, and covered her mouth.

"Oh my! Sarah will need her silkie. I've got to get it to her!" Fueled by grief, the impulsive thought was translated into words and quickly became mindless action. Rachel jumped up, climbed out of the shelter, and peered out the closet door. When she was certain the soldiers had left, she raced from the building.

I must reach them, she thought as she weaved in and out of the crowd. Workers, too tired to care, were headed out for another grueling day of slave labor at factories and freight yards. They didn't hear the voice, but she did.

"Their fate is not yours."

Rachel ignored the message but checked her pace when she heard the voice. *I must not draw attention to myself,* she thought and slowed to a determined walk. *They will be taking them to the concentration point, to the trains, but there's no way to know how long they've been gone.* Tempted to break into a run, she began counting doors in order to maintain an even, steady gait. She was up to forty-eight when she turned the corner and was grabbed from behind.

Rachel struggled against her captor. His right hand was clamped over her mouth, and his left arm pinned her back against his chest. "Rachel, they're gone. There's nothing you can do." The familiar voice was firm but gentle. "Now, if I loosen my grip, will you promise to turn around and let me hold you properly?"

As she nodded, Avram felt the tension drain from her body. He released his hand from her mouth and relaxed his hold on her. She turned to face him, her eyes swollen with grief. He wrapped his arms around her in a tender embrace.

The Belly of the Wolf

It was a rare sight. Extraordinary. Unprecedented. And for this particular German soldier—profound. He was accustomed to the sobbing and wailing. His ears had grown deaf to the pathetic cries. Their desperate shoving, grabbing, and clutching revolted him. To the Jew that moved too slowly, he dealt a harsh blow with the butt of his gun. They were animals, and he, the herdsman. But the scene that was unfolding in front of him challenged that belief.

In the midst of the chaos, the soldier saw a calm, orderly procession: forty-eight rows of four children, each with knapsacks on their backs, marching toward the train. A boy in the front proudly carried the orphanage flag. The old man who led them held a child with each hand. And they were singing! An anthem of some sort.

The soldier's eyes met the eyes of the bald man. Beyond them, the guard saw compassion, pride, and dignity. For a moment, the look penetrated the hatred that had transformed man into monster. His gun fell to the ground.

When they reached the train, the doctor and his devoted assistant calmly helped each child into the crowded car. The uncanny strength of the children and their leaders quieted the rest of the group that waited to board. A loud silence prevailed.

The train car creaked and rattled as it headed east. Its occupants stood, their bodies pressed tightly against one another. Sweat and other bodily fluids mixed with the oppressive heat, creating a pungent human stew.

The relentless rush of the wheels drowned the soft cries of the children. In a corner of the car, a man held his trembling wife. Her delirium spent, she spoke her last words.

"The wolf has swallowed us, Samuel."

The Stalker

"Sarah, why can't you hear me? Come here. Don't get on that train!" The moment Rachel reached for the child's hand, she vanished.

Rachel sat up and looked around. *Where is Elizabeth? And Hannah? Their mattresses should be right … Wait a minute. My sleeping room is much bigger than this. It's the walls; they're closing in on me!* She crawled into a corner and crouched, her hands covering her head. Beads of sweat trickled down her back as she waded through disoriented waters of consciousness toward a voice.

"Rachel, it's me, Zivia. We're in one of the rooms in the bunker on Mila Street. Take my hand, and I'll help you to the table. We'll share some lemonade and sunflower seeds."

"Is it day or night? I can't tell," said Rachel as she stared at the dingy walls.

"It's easy to lose sense of time underground. It's midnight. Avram stayed until just before curfew. He sat by your side for several hours. He didn't want to leave when he did, but he had to go secure his aunt's apartment." Zivia chose her words carefully. "He is quite fond of you."

"He's all I have now," she said and returned to the table, "and I'm all he has, now that his Uncle Samuel and Aunt Giena have been taken."

Zivia uncovered a plate and pushed it in front of her. "Please eat. You need your strength."

Rachel nibbled on a cheese sandwich. "Thank you. I know that cheese is hard to come by. You have your connections, just like . . . " His name stuck in her throat.

Zivia pulled a piece of paper from her pocket and set it by the plate. "Do you remember passing out?"

"I passed out?" A sense of disbelief thickened her confusion.

"Yes, and this fell on the floor when Avram carried you to the bed."

Rachel gasped. "It's the note that Dr. K. hid under the rug. I never had time to read it."

"No one has read it then."

If I read this note, then all of this will be real. "I don't think I can read it. Would you?"

"It would be an honor."

Dearest Rachel,

Today, our journey here ends. But a new one begins. There is, indeed, a beautiful existence on the far side of the sea, a light on the other side of darkness. Soon we will bathe in that light and be made whole once more.

Your journey here continues, my brave little knight. Never lose the hope that you so masterfully inspire in others. Let it sustain you in the lowest of times. And may it afford you the courage necessary for all your endeavors. Shalom.

"An extraordinary man." Zivia folded the letter and handed it to Rachel. "Wise in many ways."

"I should have warned them. We could have hidden."

"Where could you have hidden 193 children?" She took Rachel's hands in hers. "Guilt is a natural response, but it is destructive. It will stalk you and destroy every shred of hope within you. When the feeling surfaces, acknowledge it and then rise above it. I can't think of a better way to honor Dr. Korczak."

"How? How does ... How do you do that? Rise above feelings of guilt?" Rachel's words were strained.

Zivia picked up the letter. "Keep this with you at all times. When you are overwhelmed with guilt, read what he said about hope. Take his words and turn them into a personal prayer. It will empower you."

"I'll try." Rachel took the letter and put it in the pocket of her knapsack. When she sat back down, she sipped her lemonade, began cracking sunflower seeds, and gazed at the clutter. It lined the walls, covered the table, and filled the space under both beds. "Are you living here now?"

"Yes, and the clutter you see in this room is mine. Remember my nosy neighbors? Well, I grew increasingly uncomfortable with their endless questions, so I began looking for another place. This bunker was built long before we Jews were imprisoned here. The owners are people from Warsaw's underworld. They have invited our group and other fighting squads to live here. A few have moved in, and I suspect that we'll all be here in the near future."

"Is it big enough to hold all of us?"

"It runs the length of three city blocks. One long hallway with many rooms off to the sides. I'll give you a proper tour tomorrow. During raids, it is the safest place to be. Speaking of safety, I think it is best for you to move in with me. The deportations continue, and people without work are prime targets. Will you consider it?"

"I don't think a better offer is likely to come along." Rachel managed a smile.

"It's settled, then. We'll work on this bit of living space tomorrow, after my early morning appointment. Don't be alarmed if you wake up and I'm gone. In fact, you should know from the beginning that my schedule is unpredictable."

"I'm quite indepen ... " Rachel stopped, overcome with embarrassment. "Well, I'm usually independent. I don't make a habit of crouching in corners."

"Rachel, this place brings out the best and the worst in all of us. The strongest warrior faces moments of weakness. You are recovering from shock. I don't know many fourteen-year-olds that could face what you've faced and still have such a tenacious spirit." Zivia got up from the table and moved to the bed. She glanced at her watch. "It's one o'clock. We should get a few more hours of sleep. Tomorrow will be a big day for both of us."

Rachel returned to her bed, her thoughts jumping from point to point like a pinball. *I'm an adult now. I don't ever want to dream again. Resistance—what else can I do to help? Am I afraid to die? I'll never see Sarah again. I should have been there with her.*

The stalker returned; guilt tossed and turned in her stomach.

Determined not to wake Zivia again, Rachel closed her eyes and summoned the doctor's words. "*In the lowest of times, may hope sustain me. Let it afford me the courage I need for all of my endeavors. In the lowest of times, may hope sustain me. Let it afford me the courage I...*"

A Stirring in the Cemetery

The next forty-two days were grueling. With no work permit, Rachel was forced to spend the daylight hours in the bunker. Warsaw's Jews were disappearing by the thousands. During working hours, the elderly, the young, and the jobless were dragged from the streets and apartment buildings. Some were too weak to survive the long walk to the trains. Like a predator that patiently watches the herd and waits for the weary straggler, the *malekhamoves* was rewarded.

The mass deportations resulted in the union of fighting squads, and toward the end of the first expulsion, the resistance group had planned and executed its first missions. Acts of sabotage were carried out; construction materials and other supplies produced for the Germans were set ablaze. Retribution was imposed on the Jewish police force for assisting the Germans in the deportations. This sent a powerful message to other Jews. But after the loss of two leaders and the discovery of a cache of weapons, further attempts at organized resistance were postponed.

Rachel learned of these events after the fact. "Did you know about them?" she asked Avram one evening as they headed to the cemetery.

"Only knew about one of them," replied Avram. "The Germans need crates for transporting their weapons. Well, Marek and I set fire to a load of them at the carpentry factory."

Rachel's eyes sparked with wonder. "What an exciting operation! I'd love to do something like that. I'm bored these days. I'm going to ask Zivia for an assignment. There's not much to do during the daylight hours in the bunker."

"Just make sure you stay put during the day. Word has it that more than two hundred thousand of us have been taken. You don't really notice the loss after hours. But I can sure tell as I walk to and from work. The absence of the elderly is especially eerie."

"Two hundred thousand ... gone?" A mixture of disbelief, rage, and sorrow assailed Rachel like fierce waves crashing against a rocky outcrop. "The organization should retaliate!" Then her voice exploded. "Why wait?"

Avram grabbed her and pulled her into a shadowy passageway. Her face was flushed with rage. He hugged her tightly and tried to console her. "It's maddening. I know. But we don't have the weapons or people we need to launch a full-scale attack. The time will come, though. It will. We're all working our hardest to make it happen. Listen ... " He stopped and weighed his words. "Those of us working on the tunnels have a plan. When we collect enough, we're going to put a mound of explosives in the tunnel under the gates. Won't that surprise the devils?"

Hearing specific plans for their defense made Rachel feel a little better. And she appreciated the risk he had taken on her behalf; she knew that he was not supposed to reveal this sort of information to anyone.

"Now, shall we continue? It's a pleasant evening, and you need the fresh air."

The cemetery was full. It had been for the better part of a year. The only usable space that existed within its boundaries was between the graves. These small areas had become as hallowed as the graves themselves, for it was there that vegetables were grown. Rachel and Avram were picking green beans when they heard something stir.

"Pssssst." The sound leaked into the air.

Avram motioned for her to remain quiet. Then he slid in front of her, holding onto her from behind. He began to back up toward the gate.

"Please, I mean you no harm." An emaciated figure emerged from behind one of the gravestones. "I've escaped from the camp in the east, and I'm weak with exhaustion and hunger. I cannot make it back to my apartment tonight. Can you shelter me?" Using the stones for support, he stumbled toward them.

"Stay where you are, stranger." Avram opened the gate for Rachel then followed her through. The latch clicked, and he turned to face him. The man had slumped against the side of one of the markers. His ashen skin and the gray rags in which he was dressed made him seem like an extension of the stone.

"Who are you?" asked Avram.

He stared at his forearm before he replied. "I am J12857, a subhuman, fit for nothing but extermination. I have polluted ... " His hollow voice died in the midst of the beckoning graves.

Avram turned to Rachel. "Stay here. I am going back in to find out more about him. He is too weak to be an immediate threat."

Rachel nodded. "Be careful, Avram. He's crazy, a *meshugener!*"

Avram stepped inside and tried to learn more about the strange man. "If you cannot talk sensibly, I cannot help you."

"When we get off the train, we exchange our clothes for these *schmattes,* taken from the bodies of the dead." He looked at the stained rags that hung from his body. "Then our heads are shaved. Females too."

Rachel gasped as she imagined Sarah without her floppy curls.

"You asked my name." He showed Avram his right forearm. "Our names are replaced with numbers that are branded into the flesh. Before J12857, my name was Jurek, son of Yitzhak."

Fiery tears stung Rachel's face as she listened to the ghastly news.

"They said we would want for nothing." Jurek turned to Avram and confessed. "At Treblinka, I wanted for nothing but death."

Avram was lost in stunned silence. His eyes were still fixed on the number. The *J* seemed to be moving. Writhing like a snake. It was Jurek's hoarse cough that revived him.

"My friend and I can help you, but there are conditions."

Jurek sighed. "I have no money."

"We do not want money." He paused and turned toward Rachel. "Do you have your scarf?"

"My scarf? What for?"

He whispered an answer. "To blindfold him. I believe Zivia would shelter him in return for news, but we can't reveal the location of the bunker."

Rachel left the cemetery first. Avram had sent her ahead of them to alert Zivia. Rachel was cooking the green beans when they arrived. Avram snuck up behind her and whispered in her ear. "I could get used to spending evenings with you."

"So, what's the plan?" She turned to face him. "For Jurek, I mean." She grinned as she caught the wistful look in his eyes.

"He is telling Zivia about everything that happened to him after getting on the train. We will feed and shelter him for a few days, then take him to Emanuel Ringelblum, the historian."

Rachel had heard about Ringelblum. He was secretly recording the day-to-day struggles of life in the ghetto: the ordinary and the extraordinary, the tragic and the heroic, the sacred and the profane.

"It's hard to listen to Jurek," admitted Rachel as she spooned green beans and chunks of potato onto plates.

Avram sliced the bread and sighed. "I know what you mean."

False Security

I wouldn't make a very good thief, thought Rachel as she hesitated. *I've taken valuables from corpses, but this feels different.* She knocked one last time on the door of the abandoned apartment to make sure. No answer.

The door opened too easily. Rachel stepped inside and looked around. This particular complex had housed some of the wealthiest Jews. *No sign of wealth here. Rubinstein was right; all are equal in the ghetto.*

Rachel grabbed the hats and scarves that hung on the rack behind the door. She dropped them into her bag then walked to the couch. "Zivia said to check the underside of the cushions," she mumbled. The first two held nothing but batting, but the third one felt different. "This one is heavier." She ran her hand along the piping that lined the edges and found a slit in the upholstery. "Yes!" The exclamation snuck out and startled her. She clapped a hand over her mouth and glanced around. She didn't see him, but he saw her.

The door no longer shut properly, and he was watching her through the crack. He knew she was about to find a treasure, a treasure that he intended to have.

Rachel pulled a pocket watch from the cushion, held it up, and admired the golden shimmer as it revolved. The boy coveted it. One second he saw the watch, the next—milk, butter, and eggs. She was rooting around in her bag when he made his move.

Hands smaller than Rachel's seized the bag and pushed her down. Then he darted out the door, his treasure clutched tightly in his arm. Cursing her carelessness and the snatcher's audacity, she got up and ran down the hallway then into the stairwell. She stopped on the landing, listened, and heard the heavy thumping of his bare feet as they fell on the steps. She was gaining on him when she heard him squeal.

"Where do you think you're going, you little imp?"

Rachel stopped and held her breath.

"And what is this?" The policeman's voice swelled with sadistic delight as he examined the pocket watch. "This is my payment, right? Payment for not turning you over to the Germans."

"But you're a J—" The boy stopped. His words and his innocence faded like smoke on the wind. "There's a b-b-bigger girl on the fourth floor. She has n-nicer things. Things you'd like better. She'll be leaving the building soon. Please let me … "

"Do you think I'm that stupid? Take your filthy hats and scarves and crawl back to your hole. The

Germans will sniff you out soon enough." He threw the boy to the ground, adjusted his yellow armband, and walked off, confident that his employment by the Germans had earned him immunity from their sinister plans. He was wrong.

Back on the fourth floor, Rachel continued the hunt for valuables. She didn't want to return to the bunker empty-handed. Despite her misfortune with the pocket watch, the plunder was decent: a jar of jam, several pencils, a string of pearls, six candles, and a gold coin. She was rummaging through a chest of drawers when she remembered her second assignment.

Warning:
Retribution is being carried out
against Jewish policemen
who assisted the Germans
in the relocations.
We will not tolerate betrayal.
The *Zydowska Organizacja Bojowa*
The Jewish Fighting Organization

"Payment!" Rachel muttered, her tone dripping with disgust. "I hope this haunts his dreams." She tacked the last notice on the front wall of the post office with a little more force than necessary and headed back to the bunker.

"Yes, it seems that the deportations have stopped, but remember, the enemy is cunningly deceptive. And I believe that bringing the deportations to a supposed end is part of the deception. They want to create a false sense of security." Zivia's words were followed by nods of agreement.

"I have had the opportunity to talk with an escapee. His name is Jurek. He, like the rest of our brothers and sisters, was forced on the train and taken to the east. What he witnessed is unspeakable." She paused to clear her throat. "There are precious few who were able to escape. Of the lucky ones, some have returned to their ghettos, and some have gone into hiding. The rest have been ... " Her voice trembled and then broke.

The naked truth signaled a numbing silence. In that unholy moment, it seemed that flies stopped buzzing, the stars lost their luster, and to the east, a black ribbon of smoke curled endlessly in the sky.

The news wasn't a surprise; on some level, they all knew. There was no crescendo of rage. That would come later. Tears burned Rachel's eyes as she listened to Jurek's account of the hellish nightmare. It was no easier hearing it the second time.

"The enemy does not expect organized resistance. Your efforts have restored my hope. I am honored to be in your presence," Jurek concluded.

As Zivia listened to updates from project leaders, Rachel left and went to the kitchen. She sliced the apples into small slivers, arranged them on a platter, and placed a small bowl of honey in the center.

"It will be a sweet year," said Avram as he joined her. "The organization has several hundred members now, training is underway, and supplies are streaming in." He pulled her close.

She rested in the embrace. "You know, this group and the work I am doing have been my salvation. Every time I smuggle in a weapon, I dedicate it to someone I've lost."

He kissed the top of her head and released her. "How many packages have you delivered thus far?"

"Nine. Four from Sister Agnes and five from the bookstore. Tomorrow's delivery will make ten."

Avram picked up an apple slice, dipped it in honey, and offered it to her. "To the sweetest thing in my life."

Rachel smiled for the first time in several days. She enjoyed the sweet, juicy treat and gave him a honeyed kiss in return.

Back in the meeting room, Zivia closed with a tribute to the new year. "We have apples and honey for a belated Rosh Hashanah celebration. Let us recite the prayer for victory over our enemies, eat, and share our dreams for the months to come." As she led the prayer, her dark eyes radiated a hope and determination that was contagious.

"May the Lord answer you in the day of trouble! May the name of the God of Jacob protect you. May he send you help from the sanctuary and grant you support from Zion. May he remember all your sacrifices and accept your burnt offerings. May he give you the desire of your heart and make all your plans succeed. We will shout for joy when you are victorious, and in the name of our God we will set up our banners."

The Wolves Within

It was midnight when she set aside the sewer cover and climbed out. Distant lightning blazed a brilliant trail across the October sky. The cool air smelled of rain and wild onions.

Winter is on its way, thought Rachel as she crept along. *I'll spend this one underground. It might be warmer, but who wants to live underground for months? Maybe next winter the war will be over and Poland will be free. Who knows where I'll be then. Life seems to change as often as the seasons.* Her thoughts carried her all the way to the church.

After digging through the compost for the manna package, she tapped on the back door. No answer. She knocked again and waited. Just as she turned to walk away, the nun opened the door.

"Come in, child." Her voice was subdued.

"Is that soldier still here?" Rachel asked warily and looked behind the woman.

A shadow passed across her face. "He is, but he is not long in this world."

Rachel stepped inside, and Sister Agnes closed the door behind her.

"What happened?" asked Rachel.

"Liver disease. His yellow skin is telling; too much liquor for too long." She sighed. "Regrets. It's best not to collect them."

Not knowing how to respond, Rachel changed the subject. "There is a package, isn't there?"

"Yes, yes. And I have something to show you." She handed Rachel the package then pulled something out of her habit. "Didn't you rescue an infant boy from the arms of his dead mother last year?"

"Yes. I named him Isaac, after my stillborn brother. He was smuggled out of the ghetto by the Underground and placed with a childless couple. Why do you ask?"

"Well, Mother Superior and I were going through baptismal records." Sister Agnes stepped closer to Rachel and continued in a hushed tone. "During our inventory, she shared a secret with me. She pulled one of the records and told me it was false. The name on the record was Isaac." Sister Agnes unfolded the paper and showed it to Rachel.

"Are you certain this is the same baby that I rescued? Isaac is a popular name for Christian boys too, isn't it?"

"I'm certain it's the same child. Father Wachalska needed Mother Superior's signature on the document. He knew she wouldn't falsify a holy record unless she saw God's hand at work in the matter. Once he gave her the details of the child's rescue, she considered Isaac's survival nothing short of a miracle."

"Why didn't the parents just have him baptized and avoid falsifying records altogether?"

"According to Mother Superior, they promised Isaac that they would preserve his Jewish heritage. Their vow to the boy lined right up with Father Wachalska's feelings about conversion; he feels that making converts of Jewish children, especially given the circumstances of this war, is stealing lambs from another shepherd's flock."

A wholesome feeling, like the first ray of sunshine after an endless rain, seeped into Rachel's bones.

"There's more," said Sister Agnes with unbridled joy dancing in her eyes. "I've been in contact with Isaac's parents."

Rachel gasped. "How is he? He's over a year old now. I'll bet he can laugh from his belly." She smiled at the thought.

"They were so happy to hear that you are still alive. They pray for your safety every night. Rachel, they live in Lomianki, near the forest. They want you to move in with them and become a part of their family as soon as possible. They are willing to take the risk."

The idea triggered a mixture of feelings. "Oh my! How wonderf… Oh, but I can't. That would mean leaving Avram and forsaking the fighting organization." She looked to the nun for help.

Compassion and understanding were Sister Agnes's strengths. "The answer can be something along the lines of, 'Yes, I would love to, in the near future, when my mission is complete.' Will that do for a reply? I told them I would get back with them before the end of the week."

"Yes, that's perfect. I know with all I've been through, I could live on my own when this war is over, but it will be nice to have people to call family."

"No one ever outgrows the need for family, child. Even the bravest of souls need that support." The lines on her forehead bunched together in sorrow. "My soldier grieves for the family he will leave behind. He—"

"Does he grieve for the Jews he killed?" The words were meant to cut; hearing her friend refer to the German as *my soldier* was incomprehensible.

Sister Agnes's compassion was unwavering. "Like many of us, he is guilty of feeding the wrong wolf." From her studies of ancient cultures at the Catholic university, this legend was her favorite.

"What?" Rachel wondered if the nun had been sipping on something sweet and fiery.

"An Indian legend tells of an aging chief who sat down one evening with a group of children. He told them a story that is full of truth. He said, 'My children, there is a terrible battle going on inside of me. It is a war between two wolves. One wolf is full of hate, greed, and deception. The other is full of compassion, humility, and truth. The battle is a fierce one and eventually takes place within us all.' The children all had the same question for the chief. 'Which one will win?' The chief looked into the eyes of each child before answering. 'The one I feed.'"

The story and the tears sliding down the woman's cheeks muddied the waters of Rachel's confusion. She grabbed the nun's hand and squeezed. "I'm young, and there's so much I don't understand, like how you can help both of us at the same time. Or why babies die before they've taken their first breath. And most of all, why I can't find God."

"My sweet child," said Sister Agnes, her eyes brimming with faith, "when your fight for survival is over, your heart and mind will open, and understanding will come. Until then, look for opportunities to nurture the virtuous wolf within. Do that, and you will find God."

On her way back to the bunker, Rachel remembered Korczak's assignment that had led up to the previous year's Yom Kippur celebration: *Look for an opportunity to bless someone.* She thought about the day she and Avram took the book and the bundle of firewood to Aunt Giena. *And Misha gave the blanket to Isaac's mother. Dr. K. must have known about these wolves too.*

It was four o'clock when she crawled into her bed. The voice of confusion that had recently been screaming at her was now just a whisper. It was a relief to know that she didn't have to understand everything.

Whispers on the Wind

The snatcher held his younger sister's trembling hand. He knew the game was over; months of stealing and hiding had finally come to an end. They were on their way to the trains, and he felt an odd mixture of fear and relief. He was terrified of the Germans. Their appetite for brutality was endless. But at the same time, he was relieved. He was no longer the one in charge; the weight of manhood had been lifted from his ten-year-old shoulders.

"Get ready to run!" whispered a voice behind him.

Despite the ambivalence, his well-trained reflexes jumped at the words. The boy tightened his grip on his sister's hand as the first shot was fired. They darted around a startled guard as more shots exploded. And they escaped in a cloud of dust and fear as German blood stained the ghetto street for the first time.

In the attic of a nearby building, Zivia and her squad heard the shots. "Those are our guns," said the leader.

"Mordecai has made his move. He and several others were planted in the lines of people that were being taken to the trains." An undertone of righteous satisfaction bled into her voice. "Today's action is a threat to German supremacy. From this day forward, Warsaw's Jews will no longer be seen as helpless prey."

"How do we know the shots were from our guns?" Avram asked.

"Those shots came from pistols. Germans use high-power weapons like rifles and machine guns." Kazik smiled. "Taking the weapons from the fallen guards is part of the plan. They will make a nice addition to our arsenal."

The butcher shifted restlessly. "I, for one, will be glad when we have weapons for more than just a dozen of us. I do not like sitting in a hole."

"Our instructions for this mission were to hide and resist capture," said Zivia. "Securing and maintaining hiding places is critical to our success. Holes like this one are invaluable when the major battle strategy is attack and retreat. We have secured several hiding places, and when we have the opportunity, we must stock each of them with supplies."

Rachel lifted her head from Avram's shoulder. "I could help with that."

Zivia looked at Rachel and nodded her approval. "The deportations have resumed. We knew this would happen. If today's mission is successful, it will buy us more time. Plans are being made to help those organization members who are caught and put on the trains."

"How can we help once people are on the trains?" asked the chemist.

"Our couriers are spreading the word to the other fighting squads. They are instructing members to jump from the trains once they are in motion. Special tools for cutting the barbed wire stretched across the hatches are being distributed."

"Where will they go when they jump from the trains?" asked Rachel.

"Some will return to the ghetto, and some will hide in the forest. The organization is trying to set up contacts to assist these members. Rachel, I believe that in your new location, you can be of help to those who hide in the forest."

"How did you find out about—" She stopped mid-sentence and looked at Avram. He was scraping dirt from beneath his fingernails.

Zivia looked to Avram, then Rachel, then back to Avram. The look of dread on his face was telling.

He wasn't supposed to tell me. Realizing this, Zivia promptly closed the subject. "We're still working out the details. We can talk more about this mission when the plans are complete."

That evening, news of the attack rekindled the spirits of the hopeless. The hidden slowly emerged from their holes and ventured into the dusky streets for a breath of fresh air. Whispers of Warsaw's dauntless knights were carried by the wintry wind.

"The cowards ran from them!"

"This time the *malekhamoves* came for the Germans!"

"They have restored Jewish honor!"

Eight feet under the buildings on Mila Street, Zivia and her group were celebrating the day's victory. Mordecai and several other squads had joined them.

"The trains did not run today!" Mordecai's words were met with ecstatic cheers. "No longer will Warsaw's Jews be seen as witless victims! In the midst of tragedy, we have triumphed. This day, we will eat our bread together to celebrate this victory."

Dark loaves were passed from hand to hand as a psalm of victory was read.

"May the Lord answer you in the day of trouble! May the name of the God of Jacob protect you. May he send you help from the sanctuary and grant you support from Zion. May he remember all your sacrifices and accept your burnt offerings. May he give you the desire of your heart and make all your plans succeed. We will shout for joy when you are victorious, and in the name of our God we … "

As the collective voices faded, the familiar one surfaced. Its words echoed through the passages of Rachel's mind. "Follow Isaac. Follow Isaac. Follow Issac." She had closed her eyes to will them away when she felt a gentle nudge.

"Are you okay?" asked Avram, his eyes flooded with concern.

"I don't know." Rachel glared at him and continued. "I never told you this, but after Dr. K., Stefa, and the others were taken, I thought about killing myself. If I had not had you and this group, I would have. But now it seems that I'm being pushed out. You heard Zivia today. Thanks to you, she has grand plans for me ... outside the ghetto. Well, I'm not ready to leave yet."

Avram tried to put his arm around her, but she pushed it away.

"I'm sorry. It wasn't my place to tell Zivia about the invitation from Isaac's parents. But Rachel, this is only the beginning of the fight. We won today because we took them by surprise. When they return, it will be with an army of thousands. We cannot win. There is no hope for victory."

"All the more reason for us to stay together until the end." Determination stung the corners of her eyes.

"Zivia and Mordecai know that the uprising here in the ghetto is doomed. In order to keep the spirit of resistance alive, they are doing what they can to support efforts outside the ghetto. The group in the forest by Isaac's house is responsible for some brilliant acts of sabotage, but according to the couriers, they are desperate for food and supplies. They would appreciate the services of a clever smuggler. And you would be safer with Isaac and his parents. Rachel, the thought of a German laying a hand on you keeps me awake at night."

"Your concern is flattering, but my place is here, with you, Avram Adamowicz." A look of stubborn finality rested on her face as she turned and walked away.

As the Spit Flies

Senior Colonel Ferdinand von Sammern-Frankenegg stood over the bloodied bodies of eight of his men. "This is impossible!" Flecks of spit flew as he cursed his captains. "We are dangerously behind schedule with shipments, and the trains did not run today. I honored each of you with a position of authority. Yours was an easy job: tend your herd and rein them in when necessary. Jews are broken, hungry wretches, fit for nothing but slaughter. And you failed to contain them." Angry veins pulsed from the colonel's temples.

"Their guns were a surprise, sir." The eldest captain spoke but did not make eye contact.

"And just how do you think those weapons got into their filthy hands, Captain?" The question left him poised to strike. "I'll tell you how. Hell, they waltzed in, right under the noses of that lot of lazy, distracted weasels you pretend to command!"

The outburst cost the colonel. His head throbbed, and violent tremors left him unsteady in the aftermath of his rage. He shoved his trembling hands into his pockets and cringed when he thought of the possible repercussions.

"I'm going to turn around and walk back to my office. When I do, you three slugs are going to do whatever you have to do to make this nightmare go away. What cannot be verified does not have to be reported."

After a limp salute to the führer, the colonel stomped off, anxious to destroy eight of his files.

More Risky Business

Sister Agnes bowed her head and charged into Warsaw's whipping wind. She was on an errand for God, and she was determined not to let anything stop her, not even the devil himself.

She trudged through a mixture of snow and rubble. *Crumbs from the ravages of the wolves,* thought the nun. She stopped and picked up a miniscule piece of concrete. *God knows each one,* she decided. *His heart was the first one broken.* She put the fragment in the pocket of her habit as a reminder to pray for the healing of all war-torn souls.

Two blocks later, she stood face to face with one of the Fatherland's finest.

"Where are you going, Sister? Your place is in the church." He pressed into her space and was surprised when she didn't step back. He was so close that she could smell the raw onion that coated his breath.

Like a lion, he prowls around, looking for someone to devour. Sister Agnes turned her back to him and surveyed the devastation: heaps of crumbled brick and blackened walls of concrete, disjointed by German bombs. Polish orphans milling about, some rummaging through piles of debris and some wandering aimlessly, victims of the bonds of despair. Saddened by the ruins, she turned and faced the guard. "My service to God is not limited to a building with a steeple."

"Your kind are all alike." He spewed the words like vomit. "You see pain, suffering, and sorrow but refuse to acknowledge the cause for it all. Jews!" His face flushed with hate. "The Great War. The economic depression. Crop failure. The warts on my elbow, for God's sake! The Jews are to blame."

Agnes wanted to tell him that he should remove the plank from his own eye before taking the speck out of his neighbor's, but she refrained. She had been delayed long enough, and the woman would worry.

"Sir, the death bed waits for no one. I am needed at the hospital. May I resume my journey?" Hands clenched behind her back, she awaited his answer.

He stepped in front of her once again. "Not until you have been searched." It was a brow-raising answer that evoked an exasperated huff from the nun.

Even this Nazi wolf wouldn't disrobe a nun. She crossed her arms, pushing the rolled papers deeper into her cleavage.

He pointed at her head and hips with his baton. "Remove your headdress! Turn out the deep pockets in your robe!"

He fingered the headdress and pockets, feeling for irregularities; on more than one occasion, he had found illegal papers hidden in the lining of garments. "You seem to be clean, Sister." He dropped the concrete pebble, crushed it with his menacing boot, and then reluctantly stepped aside for her to pass.

She locked eyes with him and replied, "It is called purity, sir. A virtue worth pursuing."

Agnes walked past him and set a brisk pace. She patted her chest and smiled as her mother's words echoed through her mind. "Never be ashamed of what God has given you. He endowed you with all you need to be of service to him."

Irena's gesture was subtle, just a slight tilt of the head. She turned and walked away from the nurses' station, and Agnes followed. Both women disappeared into a supply closet.

"Each time I come in here, I'm reminded of the five loaves and two fish." Irena's hazel eyes scanned the shelves: three bottles of iodine, a dozen or so rolled bandages, two bedpans, a box of syringes, and a few bottles of castor oil. "How is one to care for the multitude of sick with so few supplies?" Irena's lament hovered in the air then dissolved and mixed with the dust that had accumulated on the empty shelves.

The nun took her hand and gave it a gentle squeeze. "It is easy to feel helpless in these desperate times. But remember, our Lord can turn water into wine. In his mercy, your compassion and devotion can become a powerful medication that can relieve pain and induce healing." Like raindrops upon parched ground, Agnes's words showered Irena's spirit with hope.

"News of the skirmish has reached every corner of Warsaw. I'm so thankful Rachel wasn't harmed. Is she ready to leave now?"

The lines on Sister Agnes's forehead deepened. "Rachel is torn; she longs for the bonds of family, yet she is devoted to the resistance. And to the boy, Avram. His present role will soon be fulfilled, though. The tunnels will be complete in a few weeks, and then he will be reassigned. I believe his new assignment will work in everyone's favor."

"We have made the necessary preparations. Jozef is finished with the secret room, I have secured some light brown hair dye, and we have told our neighbors that my niece is coming to live with us. Should anyone ever question our claims, we will have the papers."

Agnes smiled at her words. "The papers. Thanks be to the Father, I was able to get them here. If you will please turn around for a second, I'll retrieve them." After some twisting, undoing, and repositioning, the precious documents were transferred from one woman to the other.

Irena chuckled as she tucked the rolled papers into her bosom. "My mother always said that only a floosie would stash something in such a place."

"Well then, I guess we're both floosies." With a grin, Agnes looked heavenward and added, "I believe that God will excuse our indiscretion this time."

Irena reached into her pocket and pulled out a small package. "Please give this to Rachel. Tell her that we too have taken on an active role in the resistance and look forward to her help."

Agnes took the package and reached out to bless her when she noticed it: a dark brown freckle sitting at the base of her right cheek. She gasped in wonder; the mark matched that of Rachel's in size, color, and location.

The Charade

"Reassigned?" Rachel said incredulously. "What do you mean?"

Zivia lowered her voice. The meeting was over, but people lingered to see the article for themselves. "He's been reassigned to a nearby location."

"He would never ask to be reassigned, Zivia. What has happened?"

"He didn't ask. I told him that I needed him elsewhere, the arrangements were made, and he left."

Rachel felt the tears threaten. "But he didn't tell me. He never said goodbye."

Zivia's face softened. "We asked him to keep silence."

"How can Avram hiding in the forest further our cause?" Even though Zivia had not revealed the specific location, Rachel knew.

Zivia pulled her into a secluded corner of the bunker's meeting room. "You heard the words of the article. It praised us for our valor and sense of honor. The praise from the Underground is due. It's overdue. But if the fate of the ghetto wasn't already sealed, it certainly is now. We are working feverishly to plan for the final confrontation, but a few of us are planning beyond that. The Germans underestimate us; there will be survivors. And those survivors will need to be rescued. Avram will be helping with plans for a rescue operation."

Twin tears slipped over Rachel's bottom lashes and inched their way slowly down her face. "I guess it's time for Sister Agnes to contact Irena. From her house, I can smuggle food and supplies to the rebels in the forest."

Zivia nodded reassuringly. "Yes, it's time. They need you." She winked and added, "Avram too."

The two walked to their sleeping area. "Do you remember when Avram burned those shipping crates?" asked Rachel.

"Yes, I do," Zivia answered. "He seemed to enjoy it thoroughly."

"Well, if I know Avram, he is probably practicing his skills as a saboteur this very minute."

Under the cover of a moonless night, Rachel eased through the hole in the east wall for the last time. *You have served me well,* she thought as she stood and shook the dust from her trousers.

The shadow of reluctance followed her and crept into her thoughts as she turned her back on the ghetto. *This place is a pit of suffering, yet I'm sad to leave. For two years, fear and death have stalked me. But it was that fear that taught me courage.*

A runaway streak of lightning snaked across the capital sky. For a moment, it highlighted everything in its path. Rachel crouched in a dark crevice and took the package out of her pocket. She tore open a corner, willed her saliva glands to produce, emptied the powder into her mouth, and swallowed. She fished a lemon drop from her pocket to keep from choking on the bitter drug. Memories of Samuel, the candy man, surfaced as the sweet melted and washed away the bitterness. *Samuel was a gentle man. Like Avram,* she thought.

Rachel continued her journey and quickened her pace while she was still able. Her feet, having memorized every step from the ghetto wall to Agnes's church, saw her safely to the back door. By some miracle, she was able to raise her arm and knock, but as the nun opened the door, she collapsed.

"Merciful God! She's made it. Jozef! Irena!" Tears streamed from Agnes's eyes as she hooked her arms under Rachel's and pulled her gently through the door.

"Her legs are long," said Jozef. His eyes widened with wonder as he kneeled to pick Rachel up. He looked at her face and then looked at his wife. "This freckle … below her cheek … It matches yours, Irena."

"It is a sign that God is at work," said Agnes. "My relationship with this child has been an unfolding mystery. One that has deepened my faith." The nun clutched Rachel's limp hand.

Irena looked at her watch. "We must get her

settled and go. The weather is questionable, and we have a long ride ahead of us."

Jozef and Irena worked together to ease Rachel into the body bag. As Irena zipped, she looked up at Sister Agnes and answered the questions before the nun could ask them. "Do not fear, Sister. The same bag has delivered dozens of children into safe hands. It has slits in it for ventilation. The sleeping powders have relaxed her whole body. That's why she's so limp. The medicine was necessary; imagine making a four-hour trip in a body bag without something to set the nerves at ease."

"You will send word when she is safe?" asked Agnes.

"I promise," Irena said as she hugged the woman. "And thank you, Sister, for all you've done. We have loved Rachel since she blessed us with Isaac."

The night deepened, and the darkness held its breath as a lone wagon neared the checkpoint at the outskirts of Warsaw. Irena's thoughts were miles ahead of the weary horse. *We're bringing you a sister, Isaac. She is beautiful and brave. Like you, she has been chosen, and with God's continued protection, both of you will be living testimonies of the Jewish will to survive.*

"Halte!" The wagon lurched to a stop as a flash of lightning illuminated a stone face. "Papers!" he commanded and lifted the lantern.

Irena tried to look beneath the stony exterior for

the slightest trace of humanity. *None,* she thought and handed him their identification.

He looked at the documents then thrust them into Jozef's hand. "Where are you headed? What was your business in Warsaw?" He barked the questions as he walked around the wagon, the gravel crunching loudly beneath the unforgiving boots.

"To Lomianki, sir. Back to my farm. We traveled to Warsaw to pick up—"

"What do you have here?" He positioned the lantern in front of him and prodded the bag with his rifle.

"The body of my niece, Anna. Her neighbor was hiding a nasty Jew." Jozef's voice was laced with disgust. "A sick, nasty Jew. Typhus." He stood and spat the words in the guard's direction. "The lice that infected the Jew spread to the family hiding him. The daughter of the family played with my Anna. So, here lies the diseased body of my niece." His voice softened. "When she visited us, she loved to climb trees, even though she was a girl. I promised my brother I would bury her beneath the leaves of her favorite tree."

Jozef sat down, winded from the charade.

Irena prayed.

The guard returned to Jozef's position at the reins. The stony expression had relaxed, but what replaced it was far more heinous. "Go about your business and leave the Jews to us. We Germans will take care of the Jewish problem once and for all."

He stepped aside as Jozef signaled to the horse.

When the wagon was safely down the road, Irena turned to Jozef. "That was quite a charade, dear."

Hallowed Moments

"Our Father, which art in heaven." Rachel closed her eyes and searched diligently for the next word. "I know it starts with an *h*, but it stumps me every time."

Irena pulled the comb through Rachel's damp hair. *Working through the tangles. That must be what it feels like to have to learn the ways of another religion.* The thought made the woman admire Rachel even more. "The word is *hallowed.* It means to make holy."

Rachel considered the meaning. "Jews do a lot of that. We hallow a dozen different days as holidays and then every Saturday as the *Shabbat.* Shabbat is Hebrew for—"

"Sabbath," finished Irena as she handed her the mirror.

"It looks like caramel. I was afraid it was going to be blonde." She lifted random sections of hair and checked to see if the color was even then continued the recitation. "Sunday is the Christian Sabbath and the *s*-things ... " Rachel stopped and sighed with exasperation. She scanned her memory for the term, but it was tangled in a web of confusion.

"The *s*-things are *sacraments.* They are hallowed too."

"The sacraments are marriage, communion, and baptism. How did you know the Hebrew word for Sabbath?"

"The First Communion is similar to your Bar and Bat Mitzvah; all are rites of passage for adolescents."

"You know about the mitzvahs too?" Rachel lay on her side, her head propped up on her elbow. She caressed the clean pillow and smelled its freshness. *Perhaps soft, fresh pillows are hallowed too.*

"We started making plans for your arrival shortly after receiving Isaac. We did some research. Isn't Passover the next high holiday?"

"Yes, and the meal of remembrance is called the Seder. The items included in the meal are symbolic of the Jews' struggle as slaves in Egypt. While Christian children bite into sugary jellybeans, we eat horseradish. I used to be so jealous of my Christian friends."

"And now?"

Rachel picked up the comb and took it to the chest of drawers. "Maybe I'm still a little jealous, but now I understand the importance of remembering." The words were echoes of sadness. They reflected maturity well beyond her fourteen years.

Irena stood and pulled back the hand-stitched quilt and sheet that covered the iron bed. "We are gathering some of the special Seder items for you to take to the group in the forest. We would like to hold a Seder here too, if that's okay with you."

Rachel slid into the warmth of the bed and was

overcome with a mixture of sorrow, guilt, and gratitude. Tears spilled down her cheeks. "So much has happened. My parents. The orphanage. I would have gone in Sarah's place. Why do I deserve to live?" The question was directed to God as much as it was Irena. It seemed that neither had a ready answer.

Irena knelt and gazed into Rachel's eyes. "Our God is not doing the choosing. The Germans are. We must never let the world forget that!"

"But how can I—"

A loud squeal smothered her words. Rachel and Irena turned toward the sound and chuckled. Tiny fingers gripped the bottom of the door.

"Isaac doesn't like closed doors. Can he come in now? With a little coercion, he'll probably go right to sleep. If not, I'll take him to bed with me."

Rachel jumped up and went to the closed door. She sat down, gently grabbed a finger, and wiggled. Isaac's squeal stopped abruptly, and he pulled his fingers back. Seconds later, overcome with curiosity, the fingers reappeared. This time Rachel grabbed a finger on each hand, and Isaac giggled. It was a glorious, almost forgotten sound, full of healing and hope.

Irena stood back and watched until Isaac tired and resumed his fussing. She opened the door slowly and swept the toddler up in her arms. Jozef stepped inside the room and apologized. "Sorry, ladies. This little man thought the two of you needed his attention."

Isaac put his hands on Irena's cheeks and squeezed. She whistled. A smile flanked by deep dimples spread across his face.

Rachel tousled his dark curls. "I told Dr. K. you would learn to whistle like the wind. Watch and learn, little one."

"Shall I get their milk, Irena?" asked Jozef.

"Yes, thank you, dear. I'll get him ready for bed while you do that."

Rachel watched as Irena changed his diaper. "He showered me a couple of times during the week I cared for him. Has he ever gotten you?"

"Oh, yes. Many times."

Rachel tickled his belly and felt the laugh as it worked its way out of his little body. "I love to hear him laugh. It's the sweetest sound in the world."

When Irena finished with him, the toddler rolled over and crawled into Rachel's arms. She swung him around and fell into bed with him. Lying face to face, he reached for her cheeks and squeezed. She whistled as Jozef walked back into the room.

"You called?" He handed Rachel a cup of milk and Isaac a bottle.

"But I had milk last night," said Rachel.

"And you'll have milk again tomorrow night." Jozef tucked both children in and put his arm around Irena. "As long as I add a few oats to her mix, Clementine doesn't complain."

"In the ghetto, milk was as precious as gold." A fond but distant expression surfaced as she shared the story. "Twenty-six cows were smuggled into the ghetto once. The guards were paid to look the other way. Some kind of pipe system was engineered, and fresh milk flowed into hidden containers. After that, Stefa was able to get three gallons a week for the orphanage."

"That's absolutely brilliant," said Jozef. "I hope these stories are being documented. A story like that will be a bright spot in a sad history."

Rachel picked up the empty bottle that had fallen to Isaac's side and handed it to Jozef. "I will stop and thank Clementine for the milk on my way to the forest tomorrow morning."

Irena bent down and kissed Rachel's forehead. "I have a few more things to add to the bundle before I go to bed. I will leave it on the table when I finish." She stood and started to walk out then turned. "Please wake me and let me know when you leave. I know that you are a master at your trade, so I promise that I won't hover. But I'll feel more secure if I know what time you left the house."

"I will," promised Rachel.

She snuggled up to Isaac, put her arm around him, and smiled as she slipped thoughtfully into the abyss of sleep.

Secrets

The forest was alive with secrets. Not slimy, slippery secrets, waiting to spring on the unsuspecting intruder. And not wide-eyed, feathered secrets, perched in the clefts of slumbering trees. These were tired, miserable, hungry secrets. Secrets driven into hiding by the vicious claws of hatred.

Guided by the sparse light filtered through the canopy of trees, Rachel searched for the last two markers: a broken wagon wheel jutting out from a hollow at the base of an aged conifer and the dried carcass of a horse. Each time she made a delivery, the forest looked different. The markers were always in the same place, but everything around them seemed to be caught up in a continuous cycle of change. *I suppose it's the way of nature.* The thought bloomed in her mind as she stopped to look at the new buds on some old berry vines.

There were no paths to follow; the rebels worked tirelessly to conceal their presence. To Rachel, the forest always appeared undisturbed. When she reached the carcass, she stopped to adjust her bundles and to listen for the slightest sign of human existence.

A pure and delicate sound, untouched by the outside world, ushered in the bliss of dawn. "Birdsong!" The exclamation sprang from her spirit before Rachel could cage it. She ducked behind a tree and held her breath. *Out of the ghetto for two months, and my wits are already dull.* She closed her eyes and listened beyond the distant chirping of the birds.

Angry boots slapped the concrete as the SS unit approached. Kazik pushed the alarm button and grabbed the fuse. He watched intently, waiting for the precise moment. *When they reach the Brushmakers' gates, they will breathe their last breath.* Anxiety pulsed through his gut, but his resolve was unwavering.

The explosion was deafening. Vibrations shook the command post where he was sheltered. He stood paralyzed with disbelief and watched German order and supremacy disintegrate. Bodies flew, screams pierced the morning air, and the survivors ran for cover, leaving their dead and wounded behind. Kazik and Hanoch, his commander, shook themselves free from their trance and disappeared in a cloud of smoke, dust, and retribution.

Thoughts swirled in Rachel's mind as she listened. *No noisy Germans. No cries of anguish. No death whispers. The forest is full of sounds: squirrels scampering from branch to branch, the rustling of undergrowth from hidden creatures foraging for food, and the hooting of owls. Wholesome sounds, forgotten by the hopeless souls of the ghetto.*

While she waited for her contact, Rachel prayed for Zivia, Kazik, and the other squad members. "May the Lord answer you in the day of trouble. May he give you the desires of your heart and make all your plans succeed."

May he answer us in the day of trouble. May he give us the desires of our heart and make all our plans succeed. The words repeated themselves in Kazik's mind and heart as he settled into his second post. He checked his supply of bullets and grenades while he waited.

"Rachel." The whisper sprang from a crack in the ground. Ten feet behind her, the crack widened and the voice grew. "It is morning again, and God is good. He has sent me a beautiful angel bearing gifts of life."

She grabbed her bundles and crawled through the undergrowth toward the voice. Avram was waiting to help her out of the brush and into the clearing.

"You've been practicing your lines, haven't you?" Rachel reached for his hand and was pulled into a sweet but dusty embrace.

He looked into the deep brown of her eyes and answered. "I confess. When I'm not blowing up railroad tracks or foraging for food, I am thinking of you, and sometimes I'm thinking of you even when I'm doing those things."

He stood back and studied her hair. "I will need to adjust the color in my daydreams. Brighter but every bit as lovely."

She snickered. "What a character I've fallen for! My father would be proud."

He pulled her back into his arms. When he closed his eyes, Rachel anticipated a kiss. Instead, he sank to his knees, weak with exhaustion and hunger.

"When was the last time you ate?" Rachel folded her coat and propped it under his head. She felt his forehead. "No fever, but you are pale."

"Yesterday. But they didn't stay down long. Mushrooms." His face contorted with disgust. "Some aren't edible."

She opened one of the bundles and pulled out two cornbread muffins, dried apples, and honey. "Drink a little of this water first. Irena flavored it with wild mint. She says that mint will soothe an upset stomach." Rachel helped him to a sitting position and gave him the canteen.

"I shouldn't eat both of these," he said, looking at the corn muffins. "The others are just as hungry."

Rachel unpacked the remaining provisions. "I have eleven more for your comrades, Avram. Some dried apples and honey to share too." She sat next to him and picked up a cloth pouch from the collection. "And the eggs," she said as she loosened the string and poured, "are compliments of Inka and Lilka, Irena's hens."

"Boiled eggs! What a treat!" He washed down the last of the second muffin with a swig of the water and lay back down.

Rachel picked up an egg and started peeling it. "The eggs are for you. The protein will give you strength."

"News would strengthen me. It's been a week since I've heard anything from Zivia or Kazik. They expect the Germans to return any day."

"I've been praying for their safety and success," said Rachel and handed him the precious eggs.

"We've been working on dugouts for any survivors that come to the forest. They will be too weak to shelter in the trees. Besides, they make miserable beds."

"You've hidden them well. I haven't seen any evidence of hideouts."

"You shouldn't. The displaced dirt is spread throughout the forest and covered with pine needles. Then a barn door is fitted onto the hole for an entrance. To conceal the door, a thick bed of pine needles is attached. The bunkers are primitive, damp, and musty, but they're safer and more comfortable than the trees."

"Tunnels in the ghetto and bunkers in the forest. You've become quite a specialist."

Avram's eyebrows furrowed with concern. "The tunnels in the ghetto. I hope they work according to plan."

Flames of the devil's own design surrounded the building. Smoke billowed into the attic, forcing the fighters from their post. Kazik, dressed in a German uniform, called upon the powers of pretense. With a semi-automatic rifle pulled from the body of a German soldier, he led his group of "prisoners" out of the building. "Hang your heads," he reminded them. "We are a full city block from the tunnel entrance. The tunnel will take us to the bunker I found."

Rachel watched as the group of rebels ate and exchanged stories of sabotage, success, and failure.

"The bridge blew, and the steering wheel of the truck landed five feet from where I was hidden." The young man's features were still glowing with triumph.

"The railroad track into Warsaw had just been repaired." A sarcastic grin spread across the man's face. "I was kind enough to wait until the repairs were complete before blowing it up. Didn't want to rob anyone of their sense of accomplishment."

A tall brown-haired woman dressed in men's trousers spoke up. "I lured the officer at the train station in Warsaw out of his office. While the office was empty, my partner snuck in and copied the delivery schedule for the next two weeks. I can't wait to watch the liquor shipment burn."

"You couldn't have been dressed in those trousers when you did your luring," joked another woman.

The remark triggered a round of laughter from the weary band of rebels.

"When I'm not camouflaged, I can turn heads," replied the first.

"War," commented the quietest of the group. "It conceals beauty. When this nightmare ends, we will all have keener eyes for what is beautiful." Heads nodded at the truth in the quiet man's words, and the group fell silent.

Rachel handed out the last of the dried apples then passed the honey around. "The same person who helped me smuggle weapons into the ghetto told me to look for the sweetness of God in the midst of the war. May all our eyes be opened."

"Thank you for coming," said Avram and kissed her softly on the lips. "You have made this assignment bearable. I would be utterly miserable without your visits."

"Miserable, yes. Utterly miserable? I don't think so." She kissed him back. "You have too much fun blowing things up."

Tragedy and Triumph

General Jurgen Stroop stood, bloated with arrogance, and surveyed the destruction. The smoldering remains of buildings set against the dusky sky were like trophies lined on a shelf; each was a tribute to his ruthless success. Heaps of scorched rubble, laden with corpses and various body parts, sent shivers of delight through his Aryan bones. The smell of burned flesh exhilarated him. He raised his arms, shook his fists in triumph, and proclaimed, "The Warsaw ghetto is no more!"

Outside the ghetto, a truck pulled up to a manhole cover and stopped. Kazik got out and dropped to his hands and knees. He whistled into one of the three holes in the thick iron lid.

His comrades stood watch as he helped a wretched group of fighters from the sewer tunnel. "Quickly now! Into the back of the truck."

Zivia was the last to surface, her face a kaleidoscope of emotion. "You're amazing, my friend. I'm beginning to believe that the earth doesn't turn without your having a hand in it."

Moments later, her relief and gratitude gave way to worry. She let go of Kazik's hand and looked back into the tunnel. "There is supposed to be one more group. We must wait."

"Zivia, their fate is in God's hands, not ours. We cannot put ourselves at further risk. When these are delivered to safety, we can come back."

Regret and uncertainty hung in the night sky like heavy clouds. Zivia forced herself to stand and look at Kazik. "Their blood will be on my hands."

Kazik's muscles tightened with urgency, and his voice twisted in anger. "Their blood will be on German hands! Do not relieve those demons of any blame. They must one day suffocate beneath the weight of it."

The truck's engine whined reluctantly. The driver made a few adjustments and coaxed it to life. Moved by fierce determination, Kazik turned to his friends. "They may have destroyed the ghetto, but they did not destroy the Jewish spirit that lived there. It will rise again!"

Reflections

"Tell me about the night you found me." Isaac's eager brown eyes followed his sister as she walked about the room, gathering and packing her treasures.

"Again? You know every detail, from the phase of the moon to the speed of the wind." Rachel smiled. She folded the embroidered pillowcase and held it to his cheek. "It's still warm from the iron. It wasn't warm that night, though. A cold wind was blowing, so I had to bundle up."

"You were going smuggling, weren't you?" His chest and cheeks puffed with pride. "You were so clever. Those dumb guards never caught you."

Rachel laid another pillowcase on the board and began ironing. "I was near the barbershop when I heard your cry. You were cold and hungry." She looked up from her task just in time to see the hint of sadness that always dulled his expression.

"My mother was dead."

"Yes, she was. But when her spirit left her body, an extraordinary thing happened."

His smile returned. “Her spirit found you and led you to me.”

“I wrapped you in—”

“Misha’s blanket, the one with the bunnies on it.”

“When I got you back to the orphanage, Dr. Korczak examined you from head to toe.”

“He said I was strong, didn’t he?” Isaac looked expectantly at Rachel, but he knew he would have to wait for the answer. She always had to clear her throat before giving it.

“He said it was your strength that saved you.” Rachel wiped a tear from her eye, folded the pillowcase, and laid it in the trunk. She smiled at the growing collection that was her trousseau.

“I stayed with you a few weeks before you smuggled me out. That dirty place was not fit for babies, was it?”

“It was full of lice and disease, hunger and suffering. It wasn’t fit for any human, especially babies.” The memory made her head itch and her stomach churn. “So Dr. Korczak gave you some medicine to make you sleep, and Stefa packed you up in a potato bag. She put some soiled clothes on top to fool a guard in case I was stopped.”

“And it worked, didn’t it? You told the guard that your brother was sick with the ghetto disease and that your mother sent you to the dump to get rid of his germy clothes.”

“It worked. The Germans were mortally afraid of typhus. They kept their distance from anything they thought might be infected. So when the soldier dismissed me, I took you to the dump.”

"That's when the men in the garbage truck showed up to get me, right?"

"They picked you up and delivered you to Irena."

"Helping Jews like us was risky business." He shook his head for dramatic emphasis. "Smuggling was risky business."

"You've been practicing your lines, haven't you? You know all the words and have them in just the right place. You could be a storyteller … like Dr. Korczak." Rachel put the iron away and joined him on the bed.

He jumped up and stood, hands on his hips. "I'm going to be a smuggler when I grow up! Watch me leave the room without making a sound."

He held his breath, tiptoed to the door, and slipped out. When he came back, he looked crestfallen. "But there won't be any guards to fool."

"Seven years ago, right before Hanukkah, seventeen smugglers didn't fool the guards. They were shot."

Rachel's words deflated Isaac. The pride and excitement drained from his little body. He rested his limp form against her side. "How many Jews died during the war?"

She put her arm around him and drew him close. "They're still counting. The war ended three years ago, and they're still counting." She sighed deeply. "So many deaths. I don't believe there are that many fish in the seas."

"Rachel, what does it mean to be a Jew?" Isaac got up and walked to the window. He searched the night sky for the answer.

"That's a big question." She joined him at the window. "As big as the sky up there." She was combing her thoughts for the right words when her father's voice surfaced.

"History and tradition."

Of course, Father. Your passions. They will help Isaac understand, just as they helped me. Rachel opened the window and looked out on a waxing summer night. Against the velvet darkness, the stars reveled in their glory.

"Being a Jew means that you are part of a rich history. A history as deep as darkness. A history as amazing as the stars. A history that must be remembered."

His eyes widened in disbelief. "But I'm only six and a half, almost seven. How can I remember all that history? It would never fit in my head."

Rachel grinned and stroked his thick brown curls. "Nor would it fit in mine. History is not meant to be stuffed into our heads. History is a place that we visit with our hearts."

"If it's a place, then how do we get there? Can I ride my bike?"

"Your legs would turn into rubber bands if you tried to ride your bike to Egypt. We visit and revisit history through our traditions: Rosh Hashanah, Yom Kippur, Hanukkah, Passover, and the others. Do you remember what you learned at the Passover celebration this year?"

"We celebrate Passover because the malekh-whatever-his-name-was, the angel of death, passed over the Jewish houses and spared the lives of the firstborn sons. I drew a picture of him, remember?"

“The picture of the *malekhamoves* is incredible. Your talent for drawing is a unique way to remember history. Artists are powerful; they can bring history to life.”

“Will you take me to Warsaw and show me where the ghetto was? I want to draw a picture. I can see the battle in my head, but I want to stand where the fighters stood. Then my heart will feel the history.” He stopped, enchanted by the hypnotic drone of crickets. He listened until the next thought broke the trance. “The battle surprised the Germans, didn’t it?”

“It did. They underestimated our fighters. They expected to squash the rebellion and clear out the ghetto in two days.”

“The fighters kept those murder men on the run for twenty-eight days.” He turned, threw an imaginary grenade, and then ducked behind the bed. “Attack and retreat. Attack and retreat.” Rachel could see the battle that he could only imagine.

“When the end came, it was swift. Gas and flames drove our rebels from the bunkers and attics, right into enemy hands. Not many survived.”

“The ones who did escaped through the sewers, right?”

“Yes. A truck delivered some of them to the forest where Avram was hiding. They were weak with exhaustion and hunger.”

“But Avram had their hideouts ready, and you had clean clothes and food waiting.”

“We did what we could. All of us. But the rebellion was doomed from the beginning. It wasn't about victory. It was about—"

"Turning righteous anger into Jewish honor."

Rachel's words and convictions had become his own. They were etched in his mind. They echoed in his dreams.

"Next week, Avram and I will be making a trip into Warsaw. He will be checking into a job, and I will be visiting Sister Agnes. Afterwards, we could walk down Twarda Street."

"That's where you found me! Could we visit the cemetery too? Maybe some nice person buried my mother."

Rachel looked away, afraid that he could see her thoughts. *I'll not shatter his hope. He's had reality for dessert far too often.* She got up and walked to the door. "We'll talk to Irena tomorrow about our plans. Come, it's bedtime. I'll walk you to your room and tuck you in."

"Curtains open or closed?" asked Rachel as she turned down his bed.

"Open. The stars remind me of the ghetto fighters." He gazed at Rachel, his eyes brimming with adoration. "You were Warsaw's knights. And someday when you're a history teacher, I can visit your class and use my pictures to tell them our story."

What's True about this Story?

It would be quicker for me to tell you what is fictional about this story, but the history is rich and worthy of attention. Poland was invaded by Hitler in 1939. At the time, Janusz Korczak, pediatrician, writer, and radio personality, managed two orphanages in Warsaw with the help of his faithful assistant, Stefania Wilczynska. He was an influential figure and had little difficulty soliciting support for his children.

Soon after the invasion, Polish Jews were stripped of their rights, their businesses, their possessions, and were forced into ghettos. Korczak and Stefa secured a building in the ghetto for the orphanage and moved the Jewish orphans. They worked tirelessly to make life as normal as possible for the children. Korczak boarded up the windows to spare the children from brutal street scenes. The children attended classes to continue their education. They put on plays for selected audiences, secretly observed the Jewish holidays, and hosted concerts to raise money for operating costs.

The number of orphans grew steadily, in spite of starvation, typhus, suicide, and Nazi brutality.

Consequently, Korczak was consumed with securing donations for his children. The wealthy Jews in the ghetto avoided him whenever possible. He did have the support of some friends in the Polish Underground. There was, indeed, a garbage truck that made deliveries twice a week. And there were people who commented on such comings and goings. Rubinstein, the self-appointed jester, was quirky but real. Emmanuel Ringleblum, a Jewish historian, and his group of companions created documents that recorded the realities of life in the ghetto. They buried the records in storage containers designed to hold milk. These containers were discovered after the war.

To tend their emotional well-being, the orphans were encouraged to keep diaries, and Korczak modeled this behavior by keeping one of his own. *Ghetto Diary* is still in print today. Korczak believed that with guidance, children could govern themselves. So when disputes between orphans could not be easily resolved, court sessions were held.

I created Rachel and Avram, the protagonists, and put them in Korczak's care. After reading about the importance of child smugglers in ghetto life, I knew that secretly, they had to be smugglers. Children were small enough and quick enough to sneak out. They begged and scavenged, bringing bits of food back to their families. The verse at the beginning of chapter one was recited by many of them. Smuggling was risky business; if they were caught by the guards, they were executed.

There was no end to Nazi cruelty in the ghetto. "Frankenstein" really did go on shooting sprees, and he really did target babies. There was a Jewish police force in the ghetto, but they did nothing to help their fellow Jews. If they intervened, it would cost them their jobs or the lives of family members. These policemen believed that their positions were insurance against deportation. They were wrong. After helping with the mass deportations, they too were forced on the trains and sent to their deaths.

In addition to the small Jewish police force, there was a Jewish council that had been established to maintain order in the ghetto. Adam Czerniakow was the council president. He was in a precarious position; he answered to his own people as well as the Germans. During the summer of 1942, he was ordered to deliver several thousand Jews for deportation each day. He was assured that if he failed, his wife would be one of the first to die. The pressure was too much for him, so he committed suicide.

Jews who showed up at the train station, whether they went willingly or by force, were herded into cattle cars and taken to Treblinka, a death camp. They were locked in large shower rooms upon arrival and gassed. Their corpses were burned in crematoria. This *processing,* as the Germans called it, sent an endless ribbon of black smoke into the sky.

On August 6, 1942, while they were finishing breakfast, Korczak, Stefa, and 192 orphans were ordered to the train station. The doctor convinced the guards to give them fifteen minutes to prepare the children. The scene in the story, told through the eyes of the German soldier, is accurate. Korczak, with a child attached to each hand, led the lines of calm orphans to the train. A boy in front was carrying the orphanage flag, and they were singing.

Korczak's friends in the Polish Underground had secured false identification papers for him and continually tried to get him to leave the ghetto. He refused. He went to his death with the children.

Resistance fighters, underground bunkers, and tunnels. Did they exist? Absolutely. When a few precious souls escaped Treblinka and returned to the Warsaw ghetto with the dreadful news, a resistance group was formed. Zivia Lubetkin was the only female leader. Mordecai Anielewicz led a squad of fighters, and Kazik Rotem was a courier who worked on both sides of the ghetto wall. Children as young as Rachel and Avram were also involved in the resistance effort. During the planning stages, weapons and supplies had to be acquired. The fighting organization depended on people like Sister Agnes for help. She is a fictional character, but I created her after reading about Sister Anna Borkowska, a Polish nun who smuggled weapons into the Vilna ghetto in Poland.

The first skirmish occurred in January 1943 when Nazis tried to resume the deportations. Fighters were planted in the lines of people being led to the train, the signal was given, and the fighters fired on the guards. The resistance suffered a few losses, but overall it was considered a victory. The Germans retreated, and the deportations temporarily ceased. Senior Colonel Ferdinand von Sammern-Frankenegg was embarrassed and tried desperately to cover up the incident.

April 18, 1943. A few thousand Nazi troops

marched toward the Central ghetto with their tanks, machine guns, and flame throwers. Shots were fired, and so began the grandest resistance effort by Jews during the Holocaust: the Warsaw Ghetto Uprising.

The fighting organization was outnumbered, and their arsenal inferior, so they attacked from a distance then quickly retreated into bunkers and tunnels. Their weapons? Pistols, a few rifles, grenades, and homemade bombs called Molotov cocktails. As Germans fell, the rebels acquired machine guns. The bunkers and network of tunnels enabled them to defend the ghetto for twenty-eight days.

When the rebellion wasn't squashed within a few days, Colonel Sammern-Frankenegg was replaced with General Jurgen Stroop. He surveyed the situation and ordered the ghetto burned, building by building. His report, filed on May 16, 1943, declared that the Jewish quarter was no more.

Rather than being captured by Germans, Mordecai Anielewicz committed suicide when the command bunker was discovered. Zivia Lubetkin led a group of about thirty survivors through the sewers to a point where Kazik Rotem was waiting with a getaway truck. Lomianki Forest was utilized as a temporary hiding place for the survivors.

I knew that I wanted Rachel to leave the ghetto before the fateful battle. For weeks, I tried to come up with a clever way for her to leave. She couldn't just walk out through the gates. My solution came by way of an e-mail from my sister-in-law. The title of the e-mail was "Good Warsaw Rescue Story." Attached to the e-mail was an Internet article about a woman named Irena Sendler. This amazing heroine was part of an organization that smuggled more than two thousand children out of the Warsaw Ghetto, some of them in body bags! In 2007, she celebrated two significant events: her ninety-seventh birthday and a nomination for the Nobel Peace Prize. Irena died in May of 2008.

The chapter "Hallowed Moments," where Rachel is reciting the Lord's Prayer, is realistic. Many Christians risked their lives to hide Jews. To avoid suspicion, children with false identification papers quickly learned Christian prayers and traditions.

The Holocaust, one of the worst crimes against humanity, gave rise to extraordinary heroism in women and children as well as men. *Knights of Warsaw* is my humble attempt to honor the unsung hero. May their courage inspire us to become better people.

Shalom,
D.E. Cummings

Glossary

Afikomen: A broken piece of matzo, hidden and found during the Passover Seder.

Es gibt scheiBe auf dem fuBoden. JudescheiBe: German for, *There is shit on the floor. Jew shit.*

Gelibte: Yiddish noun meaning *sweetheart.*

Gotenyu: Yiddish interjection, *Dearest God!*

Hanukkah: The Jewish holiday that commemorates the rededication of the temple.

Kaddish: The Jewish prayer for the dead.

Kol Nidrei: A prayer chanted on Yom Kippur. The prayer asks for pardon for future wrongdoings.

Malekhamoves: The angel of death.

Matzo: Unleavened or flat bread used during the Passover Seder.

Menorah: A candleholder with places for nine candles.

Meshugener: Yiddish noun naming a crazy person.

Passover: A Jewish high holiday commemorating the passage of the angel of death through Egypt. Ancient Jews applied lamb's blood on the frames of their doors. The angel of death passed over these houses, sparing the lives of the firstborn males within.

Rosh Hashanah: The holiday celebrating the Jewish New Year.

Schmattes: Yiddish noun meaning *rags.*

Schutzstaffel: The German bodyguard, the SS. Shortly after Hitler became dictator, this troop of officers and guards grew to 52,000.

Seder: The Passover order of service.

Shalom: Hebrew word for *peace.*

Shammash: The ninth candle on the menorah that is called the servant candle because it is used to light the other eight candles.

Synagogue: Hebrew term for temple or church building.

Yarmulke: A skull cap worn by Jewish males.

Yom Kippur: The day of atonement.

Bibliography

"A Teacher's Guide to the Holocaust." (2005) Florida Center for Instructional Technology. http://fcit.usf.edu/holocaust/people/korczak.htm

Gutman, Israel. *Resistance The Warsaw Ghetto Uprising.* New York: Houghton Mifflin Company, 1994.

Harlow, Rabbi Jules. *Mahzor for Rosh Hashanah and Yom Kippur.* New York: The Rabbinical Assembly, 1972.

Korczak, Janusz. *Ghetto Diary.* Connecticut: Yale University Press, 2003.

Lifton, Betty Jean. *The King of Children: The Life and Death of Janusz Korczak.* New York: St. Martin's Griffin.

Rotem, Simha. *Memoirs of a Warsaw Ghetto Fighter.* New York: Vail-Ballou Press, 1994.

Scott, Bruce. *The Feasts of Israel.* New Jersey: The Friends of Israel Gospel Ministry, Inc., 1997.

Stewart, Gail B. *Life in the Warsaw Ghetto.* California: Lucent Books, Inc., 1995.

Tagore, Rabindranath. *The Post Office.* New York: The Macmillan Company, 1914.

Wood, Angela Gluck. *Holocaust: The Events and their Impact on Real People.* New York: Dorling Kindersley, 2007.